I0556393

Twisted Beautiee 5
An Erotic Thriller

Twisted Beautiee 5
An Erotic Thriller

BY

TRACY WILSON

http://beautifulpublications.com

Published by
Beautiful Publications LLC
Stratford, CT 06614

This book is a work of fiction. Names, characters, places, and incidents are either products of the author's imagination or are used fictitiously. Any resemblance to actual events or locales or persons, living or dead, is entirely coincidental.

©Copyright 2019 Tracy Wilson

All rights reserved. No part of this publication may be reproduced or transmitted in any form or by any means, electronic or mechanical, including photocopy, recording, or any information storage and retrieval system, without permission in writing from the copyright owner, except by a reviewer who may quote brief passages in a review.

PRINT ISBN: 978-1-7331792-1-8
EBOOK ISBN: 978-1-7334002-0-6

Printed in the United States of America

Dedication

I dedicate this series to my alter ego, Beautiee.

The Interviews

"Good morning..." I said as we walked into the office...

"Good morning Mrs. Osgood, Good morning Mr. Osgood..." Joselyn replied...

"Joselyn – when they get here, please escort them to the conference room..." I said as Bazil and I went into our office and I locked the door...

"Mrs. Osgood... what are you up to?"

"I just want some time alone with you... before it gets hectic..." I said as I went over to him, put my arms around his neck, and kissed him...

"Mmmm... I like this..." Bazil said as he put his arms around my waist and held me...

"Mrs. Osgood?"

"Yes Joselyn?"

"They're here..."

"Just a sec..." I said as I unlocked the door...

"I'm sorry..."

"Joselyn – you don't have to apologize..." I laughed...

"I just feel like I'm disturbing you..."

"You are..." Bazil laughed...

"See – I can't – I'ma go..."

"Joselyn?"

"Yes Mrs. Osgood?"

"They're early - are they in the conference room?"

"Yes..."

"Come with me..." I said as I took Bazil by the hand and Joselyn followed us down to the conference room...

"Good morning – I'm Beautiee Osgood, this is my husband Bazil, and this is our personal assistant Joselyn..."

"Good morning..." they said in unison...

"Thank you for coming – I appreciate your punctuality – but I need coffee – please come with us to the cafeteria – we'll be back here at 10 ish..." I said as I took Bazil's hand and we walked down to the cafeteria...

"They're here? Joselyn – why didn't you tell me?" Sheila snapped...

"Sheila – relax – we came to get coffee – we'll be back in the conference room at 10 ish..." Bazil said...

"10 ish? What time is that?"

"When my wife is done with her coffee..." he said as we sat down at the table...

"Ladies – help yourselves..." I said...

"Beautiee – I'll make your coffee..." Bazil said as he got up and went to make my coffee...

"Wow... they're so nice..." Shadajah gushed...

"I know – and Bazil is fine!" A'Licia said...

"'A'Licia!"

"What? He's fine!"

"You do know he's married – right?"

"Yes Shadajah – I'm not blind..." A'Licia laughed...

"I sure hope we get hired..."

"Me too..."

"You'll probably get hired on the spot..."

"What makes you say that?"

"You have a degree – and you have experience..."

"Shadajah – when I applied to work at Stamford Hospital – I didn't have any experience..."

"You didn't?"

"Nope..."

"Wow..."

"C'mere..." A'Licia said as she pulled Shadajah into a hug...

"I'm glad you're here..." Shadajah said as she hugged A'Licia back...

"Me too – let's drink our coffee before we have to gulp it down..." A'Licia said as they sat down at the table...

"Did you see that?'" Bazil asked as he sat down with our coffee...

"I did…" I acknowledged…

"Mrs. Osgood?"

"Yes Joselyn?"

"I'ma be in the office with my husband – I'll see you in the conference room…" she said as she left the cafeteria and went to Sam's office…

"Hey!" Sam said when he saw her. Joselyn locked the door, went over to Sam, put her arms around his neck, and kissed him…

"What I do?"

"You loved me…" she answered as she kissed him again…

"Does this have anything to do with last night?"

"It does…" she breathed as she kissed him again…

"How much time do we have?"

"10 minutes…"

"Hmmmm… okay… we better get down to the conference room… before somebody interrupts us…"

"Oh I already know…" Joselyn laughed…

"Why? What happened?"

"I knocked on the door to let them know the interns were here and I apologized because Mrs. Osgood had to unlock the door…"

"Ooohhh…"

"She said I didn't have to apologize but I told her I always feel like I'm disturbing them – and Mr. Osgood said I am!" she laughed again…

"Was he mad?"

"No Sam – he wasn't mad…"

"Well – maybe if they'd stop – you know what – never mind – let's go…" he laughed as they headed down to the conference room…

"Good morning Sam…" Bazil said as Sam walked in with Joselyn…

"Ladies – don't be nervous – this is going to be very informal – are you ready?" I asked…

"I'm ready…" A'Licia said…

"I'm not…" Shadajah said…

"Okay – I'll start with you Shadajah – what makes you think you're not ready?"

"I don't mean it like that – I just said that because I'm nervous…"

"You don't have to be nervous – maybe a little crazy – but not nervous…" Sheila said…

"Oh my God!" Shadajah and A'Licia said as they laughed in unison…

"Okay Shadajah – why do you want to work here?" I asked…

"Well… I like reading…"

"Tell me what you liked about the last book you read…"

"The last book I read was yours…"

"Really?"

"Yea…"

"What did you like about it?"

"I liked that you had a rated pg version…"

"Thank you…"

"I liked the story, and I liked the happy ending…"

"Thank you…"

"Shadajah, we publish hundreds of authors – the books range from erotic to sci-fi, to fantasy, to supernatural, to gory – what if we need you to read a manuscript that has topics or subject matters that you don't like?" Bazil asked…

"Oh that's not a problem because I don't buy everything I read – and it could turn out to be really good…"

"Hmmm… okay…" Bazil said…

"Shadajah…" Joselyn asked… "What if I tell you I need you to get me 10 ISBN numbers and 5 Bar Codes?" What would you do?'

"Oh that won't be a problem because once you show me how to do it, I'll write it down so I won't have to keep asking you…"

"Okay…" Joselyn said…

"Shadajah – I need you to set up a meeting with me, Joselyn, Sheila, and the Board of directors in the Board Room on Valentine's Day at 2pm…" Sam said…

"Okay – I'm going to book the room first – I already know you can make it so I'll call Sheila, Joselyn, and the Board members…"

"Okay – but there's an easier way to do that…" Sam said…

"There is? Oh thank God!" Shadajah laughed…

"Shadajah, do you know Microsoft word?" Sheila asked…

"Yes…"

"Do you know excel?"

"Yes – I know excel too…"

"Have you ever done a spread sheet?"

"Yes I have…"

"Okay…" Sheila said…

"A'Licia, how long did you work for Stamford Hospital?" Sheila asked…

"I worked for Stamford Hospital for 5 years…"

"Why did you leave?"

"To be honest – I was bored…"

"What makes you think you won't be bored working here?" Sam asked…

"The publishing industry is exploding – and so is the drama – and the money!" A'Licia laughed…

"You realize you'll be on the other side – right?" Bazil asked…

"Absolutely – that's why I know I won't be bored – I was on the outside for a long time – now I'm on the inside – and I can't wait!"

"There are times where it can be hectic – will you still be excited when you have to work through lunch or stay late?" I asked…

"That was a normal day at Stamford Hospital…" A'Licia laughed…

"I have a question…" Joselyn said…

"Yes Joselyn?"

"I notice your last name is Henley…"

"Yes it is…"

"Is it possible you're my cousin?"

"Huh? I don't understand..."

"My mother's name is Sheila Henley..."

"Oh my God! Really? Wow! Maybe I am!" she squealed...

"I'm gonna talk to Henley later tonight — he knows all the nieces and nephews in the family tree..." Sheila said...

"Okay — here's 10 pages from a manuscript we received recently — we found 20 errors — see how many you can find — here's your copy — here's a red marker — and... go!" I said as I sat back and folded my arms. A'Licia took her time reading the manuscript, using the red marker as she found mistakes — Shadajah read the manuscript a little faster, using the red marker as she found mistakes just as A'Licia did. When they were done, they both sat there waiting... "How many errors did you find?" I asked...

"I found 18 — that means I missed two..." A'Licia sighed...

"I found 21 — that means everybody missed one!" Shadajah laughed...

"Shadajah — we know it has 21 errors..." Joselyn said...

"So why did you say there was 20 errors if there are 21?"

"Shadajah — what I said was we found 20 errors — I never said there are only 20 errors..."

"Ooohhh..."

"Do either of you have any questions?" I asked...

"No..." A'Licia said...

"I have a question..." Shadajah asked...

"Go ahead..."

"Can I have the rest of it? It was getting good – I wanna know what happens next!" she said as we all laughed...

"Yes Shadajah – you can have a copy of the book..." Bazil laughed...

"Okay ladies – I need you to go to the cafeteria – we'll come get you after we've made our decision..." I said. We waited for them to leave before we started talking...

"I like them both..." Sheila said...

"So do I..." Sam said...

"Me too..." Joselyn said...

"I like them too..." Bazil said...

"I like them too – but there is one thing that I'm worried about..." I said...

"What?" Sheila asked...

"A'Licia said she left her job because she was bored – how can you be bored working in a hospital?"

"Maybe she just didn't like working there – this is different – and exciting..." Sheila said...

"So you think she'll work out better than Tracy did?" Sam asked...

"Oh definitely!" Sheila said...

"So do I...' Sam said...

"What if I need to give her some extra work?" Joselyn asked...

"I don't think she'll have a problem with it..." Sam said...

"We can explain that to her when we offer her the job..." Bazil said...

"Oh so we're hiring her! Thank God!" Sheila said...

"We're not hiring Shadajah?" Joselyn asked...

"Yes Joselyn – we're hiring Shadajah too..." I said...

"Oh thank God – y'all had me worried..."

"Why Joselyn?"

"'Cause I like her!"

"I like her too – she loves to read – and she found all 21 errors in the manuscript..." Bazil said...

"Can I get them?" Joselyn asked...

"Go get Shadajah first..." I said...

"Okay!" Joselyn squealed as she jumped up and went to go get Shadajah..."

"Hi Joselyn..." they both said in unison when they saw her...

"Shadajah – please come with me..." Joselyn said...

"Ummm... do you need me too?" A'Licia asked...

"Not yet..." Joselyn answered as they left the cafeteria...

"I guess I'm not getting the job..." A'Licia sighed as she sipped her tea...

"Shadajah – please have a seat…" Bazil said. Shadajah sat down… "We've made a decision – and it was unanimous…"

"Okay…" she sighed…

"Congratulation…" Bazil said as he got up to shake her hand…

"I got the job?"

"Yes Shadajah – you got the job…" Joselyn said…

"Can I call my mother?"

"Yes – you can call your mother…" I said…

"Mommy!" Shadajah cried… "I got the job! I got the job!"

"Oh Baby! That's wonderful!"

"I gotta call you back Mommy…"

"Okay Baby…"

"Thank you, thank you, thank you, thank you, thank you, thank you! I got the job! I got the job!"

"Yes Shadajah – now I'd like you to sit down so we can tell you why…" Bazil said…

"Okay…" she said as she sat down…

"First – you love to read – we couldn't have someone working here and editing manuscripts if they didn't like reading…"

"Okay…"

"Second – you were the only candidate we've interviewed that found all 21 errors in the manuscript – you impressed me with your attention to detail…"

"Third – I really like you – you're kinda quirky – in a good way..." Joselyn said...

"Fourth – I like your confidence" Sam said...

"Fifth – I like your personality..." Sheila said...

"Oh my God – thank you so much!"

"Joselyn – please take Shadajah down to payroll to meet Cheryl – and then go get A'Licia..." I said...

"Yes Mrs. Osgood – c'mon Shadajah – welcome to Osgood Publishing..."

"What's your last name?"

"My last name is Logan too..."

"Do I have to call you Mrs. Logan?"

"No – Joselyn is fine..."

"What about your husband?"

"I'm not sure – you'll have to ask him..."

"Hey Joselyn..." Cheryl said as they walked in...

"Hey Cheryl – this is Shadajah Logan..."

"I have your paperwork ready – here's your salary letter – read it and sign it – unless you have questions..."

"Okay!" Shadajah squealed as she sat down and read her letter... "Oh my God – I'm going to start at $35 thousand?"

"Yes..."

"Okay!" Shadajah squealed as she signed her salary letter...

"Shadajah – when you're done, I need you to go back to the cafeteria – okay?" Joselyn asked...

"Okay!" Shadajah squealed...

"She was cute..." I laughed...

"She was..." Bazil agreed...

"She's going to work out just fine..." Sheila said as Joselyn came in with A'Licia...

"A'Licia – please have a seat..." I said...

"Yes Maam..." A'Licia said as she sat down...

"Mrs. Osgood..." I corrected...

"Mrs. Osgood – sorry..."

"That's okay..."

"A'Licia – we've made a decision – and it was unanimous..." Bazil said...

"Okay..."

"You got the job – congratulations!" Bazil said as he got up and shook her hand...

"Really? Oh my God – when you came to get Shadajah I thought she got the job..."

"She did..."

"What? We both got the job?"

"Yes A'Licia..." Sheila answered...

"Oh my God – thank you!"

"You're welcome – now please have a seat so we can tell you why..."

"Okay..."

"First – we were impressed with your compassion..." Bazil said...

"My compassion?"

"We saw how you hugged Shadajah and encouraged her..." I said...

"Second – I was impressed with your explanation when I asked you if you realized you were going to be on the other side..." Bazil said...

"Third – I was impressed with hour honesty – when we ask why you left your last job, we don't want to hear the appropriate answer – we want the truth so we know right away if you're going to work out..." Sheila said...

"Fourth – I like how you laughed it off when we asked you about working through lunch or staying late – most people we interview hesitate or tell us they can't do it..." Sam said...

"Fifth – I like the way you present yourself – you'll fit in with the crazy..." Joselyn laughed...

"Gee – thanks..." A'Licia laughed...

"C'mon – let's go down to payroll..." Joselyn said as she got up and A'Licia followed...

"I really like her!" Sheila exclaimed...

"She was more excited for Shadajah than she was for herself!" Sam exclaimed...

"Hey Cheryl – this is A'Licia..." Joselyn said...

"Hi A'Licia – I have your paperwork – here's your salary letter – please read it and sign it – unless you have questions...

"Oh shit!" A'Licia gasped...

"Is something wrong?" Cheryl asked...

"Ummm.... Is this my salary?" she asked as she pointed to the salary...

"$45k – yess..." Cheryl answered...

"Thank you Lord!" A'Licia exclaimed as she signed the salary letter...

"A'Licia – please come to the cafeteria when you're done..." Joselyn said as she went to join Shadajah in the cafeteria...

"I'm finished..." A'Licia said as she walked into the cafeteria..."

"Okay ladies – let's go..." Joselyn said as she got up and they followed her back to the conference room...

"Ladies – please have a seat..." Bazil said. Bazil waited for them to sit down and then he continued...

"Welcome to Osgood Publishing..."

"Thank you..." they both said in unison...

"Shadajah – you'll report to Sam – Alicia – you'll report to Sheila...

"Joselyn is your supervisor. She'll train you both in certain aspects of her job because there are times when she will be giving you additional responsibilities..." I said...

"I have a question..."

"Yes Shadajah?"

"Will A'Licia and I be working on projects together?"

"That will happen sometimes – yes..." I answered...

15

"Cool..." Shadajah said as Bazil smiled...

"So... I work with Sheila – Shadajah works with Sam – and we'll also get additional work from Joselyn?" A'Licia asked...

"At times – yes..." I answered...

"And Joselyn's our supervisor?"

"Yes... for now..." I said...

"You each get two weeks' vacation, 5 sick days, and 3 personal days..." Bazil said...

"Do we get any holidays?" Shadajah asked...

"You get the major holidays – New Year's Day, Marin Luther King, President's Day, Memorial Day, Independence Day, Labor Day, Election Day, Veteran's Day, Thanksgiving, and Christmas – we don't close Columbus day, but the office will be closed this year on Valentine's Day because we'll be renewing our vows..." Bazil said as he pulled me into a kiss...

"Aww..." they both said in unison...

"Can we come?" Shadajah asked...

"You're welcome to come if you like..." Bazil answered...

"Yes!" Shadajah exclaimed...

"Included in your paperwork was a form you signed which states that you understand we have a zero tolerance policy when it comes to testing positive for drugs – if you didn't read that – please read it and be sure you understand it..."

"I did..." Shadajah said...

"Me too – that's not a problem..." A'Licia said...

"We know people use the computer for personal use at times: however, please know that all communications are monitored – that means computers, phones, texts, and tweets..."

"You monitor our cell phones?" Shadajah asked...

"We monitor company cell phones – yes..." Bazil answered...

"I'm getting a cell phone?" Shadajah asked...

"Yes – all employees get company cell phones so we can reach you in an emergency..."

"So... I'm on call?" Shadajah asked...

"Shadajah – sometimes things happen over the weekend – we may need you to do something 1st thing in the morning..." Bazil answered...

"Ooohhh... okay..."

"Okay – let's go to the bathroom now..." Sheila laughed...

"Okay!" A'Licia laughed...

"After we all go to the bathroom, you'll come with me, I'll show you where you're going to sit, and we'll get started..." Sheila said as she got up...

"Ladies – before you leave – I have one last question..." Bazil said...

"Yes?" they both asked in unison...

"Do you still want to work here?"

"Yes!" they both answered in unison...

"C'mon..." Bazil said as he took me by the hand, helped me up, and we walked back to our office...

"Thank you for calling the Business Council of Fairfield- this is Stacey – how may I help you?"

"This is Bazil Osgood for Marsha Gordon..."

"One moment Mr. Osgood..." Stacey said as she transferred him...

"Bazil – how are you?"

"I'm good..."

"That's great – how'd everything work out?"

"We hired them both..."

"Aww... I'm sure they're very happy..."

"They are – in fact - A'Licia seemed to be happier for Shadajah than herself..."

"She loves Shadajah like a sister..."

"So they've always been close?"

"Yes – I hope that's not a problem..."

"Oh no – that's actually one of the reasons we hired them..."

"Oh wow – that's great – I'm so happy you're pleased..."

"Definitely..."

"Thank you so much for calling – I'm off to a meeting – I'll be in touch..." she said as she hung up.

Chapter 2

"Come with me..." Bazil said as he took me by the hand and led me to the library. I started to turn around and go towards the living room but I changed my mind and became curious as Bazil opened the door...

"Ooohhh... Bazil... It's beautiful!" I sighed as I went in to look around...

"You really like it?"

"I love it!" I exclaimed as I threw my arms around his neck and kissed him hard...

"Mmmm... I'm glad you're happy..." he breathed as he held me. The room was painted a light, airy cream. The sofa I caught him on was gone and was replaced by two Allegro L-Desks – one on the left side and one on the right – and both desks were positioned so we could see out the bay window. Behind his desk on the left was a brown Erwin Executive Swivel Tilt Chair, and behind my desk on the right was beige Katherine Home Office Chair. There was on Alegro Computer Credenza & Hutch on my desk and there was a Brookhaven 3-piece Bookcase on the wall in front of his desk. A Dutchess Chair was in the corner near the door and on the wall in front of my desk was a paisley sand Dutchess Sofa with cream and fudge-stripped pillows. A Black Juliet Area Rug tied everything together...

"I love my chair!" I exclaimed as I sat behind my desk...

"You look good..."

"Sit in your chair – I wanna see!"

"Okay..." he said as he sat in his chair...

"I love the view..."

"I love you..."

"I love you too...

"Go sit in the chair by the door..."

"Okay!" I squealed as I go up, hurried over to the chair, posed, and took a selfie...

"Get up..." I stood up; Bazil came behind me, sat in the chair, pulled me down onto his lap, and took a selfie... "Now that's a picture..." he said as he looked at it and then he showed it to me...

"I love it..."

"I love you..." he said as he pulled my face to his, put his tongue in my mouth, and tongued me down. I tried to pull away from him but he held me by the back of my head...

"Beautiee... stop trying to pull away from me..."

"I wanna go sit on the sofa..."

"Okay..." he said as he let go of me. I got up off his lap, went over to the sofa, stretched out, and held my arms open...

"Come here my Thirst Quencher..." Bazil got up, came over to the couch, lay on top of me, and I wrapped my arms around him as we started kissing...

"I love you so much..." Bazil breathed in my ear...

"I love you too..."

"Let me make love to you..." he breathed as he kissed me again...

"Here?" in the library?"

"Yeesss..."

"I don't want to mess up the sofa..."

"You won't..."

"Yes... I will..."

"I don't care..." he breathed as he opened my pants and pushed them down off my waist, past my knees, and down to my ankles. I kicked them off my ankles and opened my legs and Bazil got up on his knees, opened his pants, took his dick out, and began stroking it... "You want this?"

"Yes..." I breathed. Bazil lay down on top of me, eased himself inside me, and kissed me as he began thrusting...

"Hmmph... Hmmph... Hmmph... Hmmph..."

"Mmmph... Mmmph... Mmmph... Mmmph..." I put one leg up on the back of the sofa, dropped my other leg down off the couch, grabbed his ass, and pushed him in deeper...

"Hmmph… Hmmph… Hmmph…
Hmmph…"

"Mmmph… Mmmph… Mmmph…
Mmmph…" Bazil put his arms underneath my
back, held me tighter, and started thrusting
harder…

"HMMPH! HMMPH! HMMPH!
HMMPH!"

"MMMPH! MMMPH! MMMPH!
MMMPH!" Bazil was thrusting harder, deeper,
and faster and he was coming with me…

"HMMPH! HMMPH! HMMPH!
HMMPH!"

"MMMPH! MMMPH! MMMPH!
MMMPH!" Bazil slowed down but didn't stop as
our orgasms subsided and we continued kissing…

"Mmmm…. You needed that…" I
breathed…

"So did you…" he breathed…

"I can't wait 'till Valentine's Day…"

"Neither can I…"

"I'm hungry…"

"You want more…"

"Always…"

"Let's go get something to eat…"

"Okay…"

"Then we'll go upstairs…"

"Okay…"

"Then I'll give you more…"

"Okay…" Bazil got up, extended his hand,
took mine, helped me up off the couch, pulled me

to him, and held me... "Thank you..." I breathed...

"You're welcome..." he said as we walked out the library and into the kitchen... "What would you like?"

"You know what – I'm in the mood for pizza!" I laughed...

"We don't have any pizza in the fridge..." Bazil laughed...

"I know – let's order a large pie – with meat!"

"Ummm... what kind of meat would you like?" he asked as he smiled at me mischievously...

"I want sausage, pepperoni, meatball, and bacon – oh – and I want some potato chips..."

"Ummm... Beautiee?"

"Yes Bazil?"

"Is there something you need to tell me?" he laughed...

"I already told you – I'm hungry!" I laughed. I knew what Bazil was asking me but I wasn't ready to answer. I hadn't had a chance to get to the store to buy a pregnancy test – I was too busy living – I was home – I had my life back – the life I always wanted. I was loving, I was writing, I was feeling like I was back on my honeymoon, we were renewing our vows...

"Beautiee..."

"Yeesss...."

"Beautiee..."

"Yeesss..."

"Beautiee!" Bazil exclaimed as he grabbed me by the shoulders...

"Yes Bazil?"

"Where were you?" he laughed...

"I was... dreaming..." I sighed...

"Musta been a hell of a dream..." Bazil laughed... "You didn't even hear me calling you..."

"It was..." I sighed...

"You wanna eat here or you wanna eat upstairs?"

"Hmmm... upstairs..." I sighed...

"Okay – we'll stay downstairs until the pizza comes... and then we'll go upstairs..."

"Okay..." I sighed as I looked out the window...

Chapter 3

"Hi Mommy!" Shadajah exclaimed as she walked inside...

"Congratulations Baby – I'm so happy for you!" her mother said as she pulled Shadajah into a hug and kissed her on her cheek... "Come sit down – tell me everything!" her mother said as she went to sit at the kitchen table...

"Okay – I'll tell you everything Mommy – but I gotta pee first!" she said as she ran to the bathroom... "You want some breakfast Mommy?"

"You wanna cook? Oh I know this is gonna be good..."

"Okay – I'ma fry some eggs, some bacon, make some toast, and we're gonna have coffee..."

"Okay!" Her mother watched as Shadajah went in the refrigerator and took out four eggs, bacon, and four slices of bread. She started humming as she put the kettle on and her mother smiled. She took two cups down from the cabinet, put them on the counter, added the coffee and sugar, and turned the flame down under the kettle. She continued humming as she took the cast iron frying pan out of the cabinet underneath the sink, put it on the stove, and turned on the flame. After she put the bacon in the frying pan, she started talking...

"Mommy – they are so nice!"

"Really?"

"Yea – and Mrs. Osgood is funny!" she laughed as the bacon started crackling in the frying pan...

"Oh yea?"

"We we're early – so Mrs. Osgood comes into the conference room and says I appreciate your punctuality, but I need coffee..."

"I like her already!"

"And then Joselyn says I'm quirky – in a good way..." Shadajah said as she took the bacon out of the frying pan, put it on their plates, cracked the eggs into the frying pan, and let them fry...

"Really?"

"Yea – hang on a second..." she said as she flipped the eggs, put the toast in the toaster, and got the butter out the refrigerator. The toast popped up, and she buttered it quickly...

"You need any help?"

"No Mommy – I got it..." she said as she turned the flame off, took the eggs out the frying pan, put them on their plates, and put the plates on the table..."

"You are so good at that!" her mother exclaimed...

"All I do is let the white part cook long enough so I can pick it up with the spatula..." she said as she turned the kettle off, made their coffee, put the cups on the table, and then sat down with her mother...

"Take my hands..." her mother said... "Lord, thank you for this food, and thank you for your many blessings..."

"Amen!" Shadajah said as they started eating...

"Okay – tell me!" her mother laughed...

"Well – we were early so Joselyn took us to the conference room..."

"Yea – you said that..."

"So Mrs. Osgood introduced herself and told us she needed coffee, and we went to the cafeteria..."

"Okay..."

"So we got coffee, we sat down, and relaxed for a little while..."

"Girl – you didn't relax!" her mother laughed...

"I tried to – A'Licia was there and that made me feel better..."

"A'Licia? Your friend?"

"Yes..."

"So wait a minute – you and A'Licia went to interview for the same job?"

"Kinda..."

"Girl!"

"Alright, alright..." Shadajah laughed... "So Mr. and Mrs. Osgood went to the conference room first, and then Joselyn came to get us..."

"Okay..."

"So – silly me – Mrs. Osgood asked us if we were ready..." Shadajah laughed... "And I said I'm not ready..."

"Why would you do that?"

"Mrs. Osgood asked me the same thing..."

"What'd you say?"

"I told her I just said that 'cause I was nervous..."

"Oh good – I'm sure she understood..."

"She did – they were really nice..."

"I'm glad..."

"So they asked me why I wanted to work there and I said I love reading..."

"So you and A'Licia were in the conference room together?"

"Yes..."

"And they asked you questions in front of her?"

"Yes – they asked her questions in front of me too..."

"Ohh... that's different..."

"I know – right? So anyway – it was Mrs. Osgood, Mr. Osgood, Joselyn, Sam, and Sheila..."

"Oh wow!"

"So I told Mrs. Osgood that I read her books..."

"You did?"

"Yes – and she asked me what I liked about them and I told her..."

"You had the job right there..."

"Nope..."

"You don't think so?"

"Nope..."

"Okay – go ahead..."

"So they asked me what if I had to read or edit a manuscript that had something I didn't like and I said that's okay because I don't buy everything I read – and even if I don't like it, it might turn out to be really good..."

"Nice!"

"Then they asked me if I knew word, excel, did spreadsheets, etc...."

"Okay..."

"And Sam asked me to schedule a board meeting..."

"On the spot?"

"Yes..."

"How did you do that?"

"I told him I would book the room and call everybody else because I already knew he could go..."

"That was smart..."

"So then Joselyn asked me what would I do if she needed me to order 10 ISBN numbers and 5 Barcodes..."

"I don't even know what that is – what would you do?"

"I'd ask her what to do, and then I'd write it down so I wouldn't have to ask her again...

"Oh – good answer..."

"So then, Mrs. Osgood gave us 10 pages from a manuscript and a red marker. She said they found 20 errors – but I found 21..."

"Oh wow! That was a trick!"

"Yep – and I was the only one to find all 21 errors – A'Licia only found 18..."

"Ooohhh..."

"Here's the best part..."

"What Baby?"

"After I called you, Mr. Osgood asked me to sit down so he could tell me why I got the job..."

"I bet it was because you read his wife's books..."

"Nope – it was because I found all the errors – Mr. Osgood said he liked my attention to detail!" Shadajah beamed...

"Oh Shadajah! That's wonderful!"

"They also liked my personality and my answers to the other questions..."

"I'm so proud of you!"

"And guess what?"

"What Baby?"

"A'Licia and I might work on some projects together..."

"I'm so happy for you..."

"Oh – I almost forgot – they're gonna be closed on Valentine's Day..."

"Why?"

"Because they're gonna renew their vows..."

"Aww..."

"And Mr. Osgood said I can come if I want..."

"Oh baby – you have to go – and take lots of pictures!"

"I will Mommy – and guess what else?"

"Yes Baby..."

"I get a cell phone too..."

Chapter 4

"Hi…" her husband said as A'Licia came in…

"Hi…" she sighed as she put her keys on the table…

"Aww… don't worry babe – you'll get the next one…"

"Babe – I got the job…"

"What? That's great – congratulations…" he said as he pulled her into a hug and kissed her…

"I'm so happy…."

"There's my girl – come sit with me – tell me everything…"

"Okay…" she said as they went over to the couch and sat down…"

"Okay – when we first got there we were early…"

"We? Who's we?"

"Me and Shadajah…"

"Oh shit – you both went for the same job?"

"Yes – and we both got hired…"

"Wait a minute… how…"

"Let me tell you…"

"Okay…"

"So – we were early so Joselyn took us to the conference room…"

"Okay…"

"So Mrs. Osgood thanked us for coming but since we were early, she needed coffee – so we all went to the cafeteria…"

"They have a cafeteria?"

"Yes…"

"Oh that's nice…"

"So the Osgoods went back to the conference room and then Joselyn came to get us…"

"Wait – you both got interviewed? At the same time?"

"Yes…"

"Hmmm… that's different…"

"First, they questioned Shadajah, and then they questioned me…

"Did they ask you the same questions?"

"No…"

"Okay…"

"So it was Mr. Osgood, Mrs. Osgood, Joselyn, Sam, and Sheila…"

"They all interviewed you?"

"Yes…"

"Oh wow…"

"So they asked me how long I worked at the hospital and why did I leave…"

"What'd you say?"

"I told them the truth…"

"You did?"

"Yup – I told them I was bored..."

"You said that?"

"I sure did..."

"What'd they say?"

"They asked me how did I know I wasn't going to get bored working for them..."

"Uh oh..."

"I told them the publishing company was exploding – and so was the drama – and the money – and that was exciting..."

"That was a great answer Babe..." he said as he kissed her...

"Babe... stop..." she laughed...

"Okay – I'm sorry – go 'head..."

"So then they asked me if I would still be excited if I had to work through lunch or stay late..."

"Shit – you did that at the hospital..." he laughed...

"That's what I told them!" she laughed... "So then Mr. Osgood says you realize you're on the other side now – right?"

"What'd you say?"

"I said I couldn't wait!"

"Babe! You nailed it!"

"Well – I did mess up one thing though..."

"What?"

"They gave us 10 pages of a manuscript and a red marker – Mrs. Osgood said they found 20 errors – Shadajah found 21 – I found 18..."

"Oh wow..."

"They didn't mind though..."

"That's good..."

"So they sent us to the cafeteria, they talked, and then Joselyn came to get Shadajah..."

"Oooohhh..."

"I thought I didn't have the job – but Joselyn came to get me when they were finished with Shadajah..."

"Oohhh... okay..."

"So Mr. Osgood told me I got the job and then..."

"What Babe?"

"He asked me to have a seat so they could tell me why I got the job..."

"Oh that's nice!"

"They said they liked my compassion, my honesty, my willingness to work through lunch, stay late, how excited I was, and how I was ready to be on the other side..."

"Other side?'

"Babe – I know a lot from social media – now I'll be on the inside..."

"Ooohhh – I have another question..."

"Okay..."

"They liked your compassion?"

"They saw me encouraging Shadajah and they saw me give her a hug..."

"Babe! That was so sweet!"

"I didn't even know they saw that..."

"They're very observant..."

"Babe – that's not all..."

"What?"

"You know at the hospital I only got New Year's Day, Thanksgiving, and Christmas?"

"Yea..."

"I get 10 holidays..."

"Oh wow!"

"And that's in addition to two weeks' vacation, 5 sick days, and 3 personal days – that's like having a month off with pay!" she squealed... "And guess what else?"

"What Babe?"

"They're closing for Valentine's Day this year because they're renewing their wedding vows..."

"Aww... that's beautiful... Babe – I'm sorry..." he said as he grabbed her and kissed her..."

"That's okay – but let me finish..."

"Okay – hurry up – I'm excited!"

"So... I went to payroll to sign my paperwork and I read my Salary Letter..."

"And?"

"Babe – I'm making more money than I did at the hospital..." she said as she started crying..."

"Thank you Lord - thank you!" he said and then he kissed her again...

"That's what I said!"

"We can start looking at houses again..."

"I know..."

"We can have a baby..."

"I know…"

"C'mon…" he said as he stood up and extended his hand to help her up… "Let's celebrate…"

"Okay…" she said as she took his hand, and   they   went   into   the   bedroom.

Chapter 5

"Good morning Joselyn…" I said as I walked into the building…"

"Good moorrrnnniiinnng Mrs. Osgood…" Joselyn sang…

"Well that was nice! What has you in such a pleasant mood – or shall I say who?"

"Everything…" she sighed…

"Okay – I need you to make me some coffee – and I need you to give me the tea…" I said as I took Joselyn by the hand and we walked to the cafeteria…

"Good morning Mrs. Osgood…" Cheryl said as we walked into the cafeteria…

"Good morning Cheryl – how's everything?"

"Good… I guess…" she sighed…

"If there's anything we can do to make your day better, please let me know…" I said as I sat down. I meant what I said – probably wasn't going to do it, but I would like Cheryl to tell me anyway…

"Here's your coffee…" Joselyn said as she sat down…

"Okay – tell me…"

"I'm finally getting some sleep…"

"That's good..."

"It feels so good to be able to say I need this done – and it gets done!"

"Oh so Shadajah's working out?"

"They both are..."

"Oh that's good..."

"I can go to lunch with my husband – I missed that!"

"I'm sorry Joselyn..."

"I'm not..."

"I thought you were tired?"

"I was – but I'm glad I got the opportunity – now I know what I bring to the table..."

"You're not leaving me... are you?"

"I'll be here as long as Sam is here..."

"Oh – you'll be here forever then..." I laughed...

"I need to get back to my office – I need to gear up for your project..."

"Okay Joselyn – I'll see you later..."

"Mrs. Osgood – I need to see you in my office..." Bazil said as he walked over to the table with his coffee and sat down...

"Am I in trouble?" I asked, smiling at him mischievously...

"Yes... you are..." he answered as he sipped his coffee...

"Oh no... am I going to be punished?"

"Yes... you are..."

"Good..."

"Good morning Mr. Osgood..." Cheryl said as she walked past our table on her way out...

"Good morning Cheryl..."

"Have a good day..." she said as she left the cafeteria...

"What's her problem?" Bazil laughed...

"She's not happy..."

"Fuck her..." Bazil laughed...

"How long has she worked here?"

"Five years – why?"

"When was the last time she got a raise?"

"Beautiee... please don't tell me you're suggesting we give her a raise..."

"That's exactly what I'm suggesting..."

"Beautiee – I love you..."

"I love you too..."

"I'm not doing that..."

"We have to..."

"Why?"

"We can't let her leave..."

"Why not? We have the video..."

"As long as she's here, we have eyes and ears on her – if we let her leave, we have nothing..."

"You're up to something..."

"Yes..."

"Tell me..."

"She's going to help me collect..."

"Oohhh... I get it..."

"I knew you would..."

"How long do we need to keep her?"

"At least the rest of the year – if not longer..."

"Why so long?"

"The longer she stays... the more comfortable she'll get..."

"Ooohhh...."

"She'll slip up and say something to somebody – if she hasn't already..."

"What are you getting at?"

"The other day – when she had her liquid lunch – she met with Tracy..."

"How'd you know that?"

"The bartender at Fridays..."

"Ooohhh... I see..."

"That's why we need to give her a raise..."

"Okay – you win – I'll agree to $5k – but no more..."

"You're wrong..."

"I am?"

"You are..."

"How?"

"We win..." I said as I pulled him into a kiss...

"We win..." he breathed as he kissed me back...

"Let's go back to the office..."

"Shouldn't we give Cheryl the good news?"

"Not yet..."

"Why not?'

"You need to punish me first..." I whispered as I got up and headed back to our office with Bazil following close behind me. When we got in our office Bazil locked the door... "Why am I being punished?"

"Why does it matter?"

"Because... if I know why you're punishing me... I may wanna do it again..."

"I want you to go over to the couch, kneel on it, and hold on..."

"Okay..." I breathed. I went over to the couch, kneeled on it, and held on to the back. Bazil came over to me, slid my skirt up, bent down, took his dick out, and rubbed the tip at the entrance to my pussy...

"You're wet..."

"Yeesss..."

"You want me to punish you..."

"Yeesss..."

"Tell me..."

"Punish me..."

"Say please..."

"Please... Punish me..."

"As you wish..." he growled as he thrust himself inside me and started fucking me hard...

"Bazil... Fuck!" I whispered (if you can call it that)...

"Beautiee... you're so fuckin' wet..." he whispered...

"Your dick feels so fuckin' good!"

"Yes... Beautiee... That's it... Shit!"

"Bazil... Huh... I'm cumming...."

"Cum all over my dick! Shit!"

"Bazil... Bazil... Bazil... Haah... Haah... Haah..."

"Beautiee... Fuck! I'm cumming! Uuuggghhh!"

"That was so fuckin' good..." I breathed...

"It was..." Bazil breathed as he started kissing me on my neck...

"I needed that..."

"So did I..."

"I guess we should do some work now..."

"We just did..."

"Pass me some tissues..." I said as I stood up...

"Here..." Bazil laughed as he handed me a box of tissues... "I'll have Cheryl come down now so we can give her the good news..."

"Okay..." I breathed as I adjusted myself and Bazil called Cheryl...

"Yes Mr. Osgood?"

"I need to see you in my office..."

"I'll be right down..." Cheryl said as she hung up...

"Le'me unlock this door..." I said as I got up to unlock the door just it time...

"Mr. Osgood?"

"Yes Cheryl?"

"May I come in?"

"Yes Cheryl..."

"You wanted to see me?"

"Yes – I'll make this quick – We're giving you a $5k raise – effective your next paycheck..."

"Thank you!"

"You're welcome – have the paperwork done as soon as possible so I can sign off on it..."

"I will – thank you!"

"You're welcome..." Bazil said as she hurried out the office...

"Hey Girl..."

"Cheryl! Why you callin' me from work?"

"I just got a raise!'

"Oh shit!"

"I saw Mrs. Osgood in the cafeteria this morning – she asked me how I was doing – I said okay I guess – she said if there's anything we can do for you let me know – next thing I know, Mr. Osgood is calling me to his office to tell me I got a $5k raise!"

"Damn – I wish I didn't quit..."

"Me too girl..."

"Be careful Cheryl..."

"Why?"

"I don't know... just be careful..."

"I come to work every day, I'm on time, I do my job... and I got a raise..."

"Congratulations..."

"Thank you girl – I'll talk to you later..."

"What are you looking at Bazil?" I asked...

"You were right..."

"About Cheryl?"

"Her phone lit up as soon as she got back to her office…"

"Mr. Osgood?"

"Yes Cheryl…"

"May I come in?"

"Yes Cheryl…"

"Here's the paperwork for my raise…" she beamed as she put the paperwork on Bazil's desk. Bazil picked it up, looked it over, signed it, and handed the papers back to her…

"Thank you again…" she said as she hurried out of the office and Bazil called Sam…

"Sam…" Bazil said as Sam answered his phone…

"Yes Bazil?"

"Cheryl just left the building…"

"Okay…"

"I need you to track her, find out where she is, go there, tell me who she's meeting with, and report back to me…"

"You think she's looking for another job?"

"Yes…" Bazil lied…

"First Tracy – now Cheryl…"

"What do you mean?"

"People don't wanna work – but they wanna get paid…"

"Exactly…"

"What are you going to do if she wants to leave?'

"We just gave her a $5k raise – hopefully that will keep her here…"

"Oh my – it should..."

"I hope so..."

"Bazil – I wanna thank you..."

"Thank me?'

"My wife is really happy... and that makes me happy..."

"You're welcome – but my wife is the one that's responsible..."

"Well – thank you for marrying her then..."

"You're welcome..." Bazil laughed...

"I found her – she's at the Bridge House Restaurant – I'll get back to you..." Sam said as he hung up...

"Is Sam as happy as Joselyn?" I asked...

"Yes he is..."

"Good..."

"He thanked me for Joselyn's happiness and I told him you were responsible, so he thanked me for marrying you..." he said as he got up, pulled me up into his arms, and kissed me...

"Thank you for marrying me..." I breathed...

"Thank you for marrying me..." he breathed as we continued kissing.

Chapter 6

"Welcome to Bridge House – may I start you out with something to drink?" the waitress asked...

"I'll have the Cabernet Sauvignon..."

"Excellent choice – I'll be back..." the waitress said as she walked away to get Cheryl's wine and Sam came inside...

"Cheryl! What are you doing here?" Gertrude asked as she sat down with Cheryl...

"I'm here to celebrate!" Cheryl exclaimed...

"Whatchu celebrating?"

"I just got a raise..."

"Here's your wine – are you ready to order?" the waitress asked...

"Yes – I'd like your BH Meatloaf..."

"What kind of celebration is that? Miss – bring her some lobster!" Gertrude laughed...

"Thank you Aunt Gert – but I really want my meatloaf!" Cheryl laughed...

"Fine – bring me the lobster then!" Gertrude laughed...

"Yes Maam – with this be separate checks?"

"Yes..." Cheryl said...

"You just got a raise and you can't treat your Aunt to lunch?"

"I'm sorry – it's not effective until my next check...

"See – that's that bullshit – they could 'a made it effective this check – that's why Beautiee got her ass beat!"

"Aunt Gert!"

"She did!" Gertrude laughed...

"I saw the video – she didn't look like she was getting her ass beat to me..." Cheryl laughed...

"She wasn't getting her ass beat on that one..." Gertrude said...

"Here's your meatloaf, and here's your lobster..." the waitress said as she placed their plates on the table...

"Oh my God! You have another video?"

"I sure do..."

"Can I see it?"

"Sure..." Gertrude said as she took her phone out and played the video...

"Oh shit!" Cheryl laughed...

"Why you laughing?"

"Beautiee ain't gettin' her ass beat – Beautiee's beatin' that ass!"

"You know what –never mind – I don't know why I bother..." Gertrude said as she went to put her phone away...

"Wait!" Cheryl squealed...

"Why?"

"Send it to me!"

"Hell no!"

"C'mon! Please?"

"I'ma send it to you – but I swear to God – if I find out you're sending this out or putting it online…"

"I'm not! I don't wanna get fired!"

"I don't either – so you better not…"

"I'm not!"

"Okay – hurry up and finish eating so you can go back to work…"

"Don't you have to get back to work?"

"I'm not working today…"

"Ohh…" Cheryl said as they finished eating and Sam left the restaurant… "Aunt Gert?"

"Yea?"

"Why'd you take the videos?"

"Shit – we always take videos of celebrities!" Gertrude laughed…

"Oh my God!"

"Calm down – we don't send 'em out or blackmail anybody – we just watch 'em and laugh!"

"I can't believe y'all do that…"

"We're locked behind bars all day – we need to do something to keep from being bored…"

"I never thought your job was boring…"

"Well – I guess my job is exciting compared to where you work…"

"Oh shoot – it's after 1 o'clock – I gotta go!" Cheryl exclaimed as she put some money on the table, jumped up, hurried out the restaurant, and hurried back to the office...

"She met Gertrude at the restaurant..." Sam said...

"She had lunch with Gertrude? That's the thanks we get for giving her a $5k raise? Fuckin' Bitch!" Bazil growled...

"I don't think it was like that..." Sam said as I came into the office...

"What's wrong?' I asked...

"I knew we should've fired her ass!" Bazil snapped...

"Honey... what happened?" I asked as I put my hand on his shoulder...

"She had lunch with Gertrude..."

"Mrs. Osgood – I don't think it was like that..." Sam said...

"What do you think Sam?"

"Well – from what I could tell – Cheryl wasn't expecting her..."

"Really?"

"I don't think so..." Sam said as Cheryl came running into the office...

"Mr. Osgood – Mrs. Osgood – I need to talk to you..."

"I'll see you later..." Sam said as he left and closed the door..."

"Is something wrong?" Bazil asked...

"Please don't fire me!" she said as she sat down and started crying...

"Nobody's going to fire you..." I said as I sat down beside her and took her hand... "What happened?"

"I went to Bridge House for lunch..."

"They have good food..." I said...

"What happened Cheryl?" Bazil asked...

"I went there to celebrate my raise..."

"Okay..." I said...

"My Aunt came to the table..."

"Oh – your Aunt met you for lunch? That's nice..." I said, pretending I didn't know it was Gertrude...

"Mrs. Osgood... you don't understand..."

"What is it Cheryl?"

"My Aunt Gertrude came to the table..."

"Ohhh..."

"I didn't invite her – I swear!"

"I believe you..."

"You do? Really?"

"Yes..."

"What happened Cheryl?" Bazil asked again, this time raising his voice...

"Mr. Osgood – I'm sorry!"

"Cheryl... if you're not going to tell us what happened – please leave..." Bazil said as he got up and opened the door...

"Wait... I'll tell you..."

"Go ahead..."

"My Aunt has another video..."

"Another video? Of my wife?"

"Yes..." she whispered...

"How do you know she has another video?" I asked...

"She showed it to me..."

"Oh my God!" I exclaimed...

"I have it..."

"You have it?' Bazil asked...

"Yes – I asked her to send it to me... so I could give it to you..." she said as she handed Bazil her cell phone. Bazil took her phone, looked at the video, and I knew what was on it by the expression on his face... "I'm sorry Mrs. Osgood..." Cheryl said as I rolled my eyes...

"Thank you Cheryl..." Bazil said as he handed Cheryl back her phone...

"Mr. Osgood... there's something you need to know..."

"What is it?"

"My Aunt said they all take videos of celebrities..."

"Celebrities?"

"My Aunt said they take videos of celebrities to keep from being bored..."

"Why are you telling us all this?"

"Because... you could've fired me... and you didn't..."

"Thank you..."

"Are you goint to report my Aunt?"

"No..." Bazil lied. Actually – it wasn't a lie – he was telling the truth – Gertrude was going to be reported – but he wasn't the one that was going to do it..."

"Thank you..." Cheryl said...

"You're welcome Cheryl – I need to speak to my wife – in private..."

"Of course – I'll see you later..." she said as she got up and left... and I closed the door behind her and locked it...

"C'mere..." Bazil said as he pulled me into his arms and held me...

"Was it as bad as the first one?" I asked...

"This one was worse..."

"Worse?"

"You stomped the shit outta her..."

"That was my first night there..."

"I'm sorry..."

"I know..."

"I'm sending this to Smalls..."

"I know that too..."

"You don't want me to?"

"I do.."

"Okay..." Bazil said as he sat down at his computer, attached the video to an email, hit send, and called Smalls...

"Another one?!" Smalls exclaimed...

"Yes..." Bazil answered...

"Where'd you get this one?"

"Cheryl..."

"What?! Why does she still have a job?"

"Because Beautiee is right about her..."

"What?!"

"As long as she stays here, we have eyes and ears on her..."

"You don't need to keep her there! Fire her!"

"Smalls?"

"Yes Beautiee?"

"We just gave her a raise..."

"Beautiee! Why?!"

"Because as soon as she got her raise, she came in here, gave us that video, and gave us some tea..."

"She gave you a cup of tea?"

"Smalls!" Bazil laughed...

"What? I don't get it..."

"She gave us information..."

"What'd she say?"

"She said they all take videos of celebrities because it keeps them from being bored..."

"Oh shit!"

"That's why I sent it to you..." Bazil said...

"Beautiee?"

"Yes Smalls?"

"What if she's playing you?"

"If she's playing us... then she'll take the fall with her Aunt... and everyone else..."

"Hello Beautiee! Welcome back!"

"Damn right!" I laughed...

"Call me when you're ready..."

"We will..." Bazil said and then he hung up... "You wanna see what we paid $5k for?"

"Sure..." I said as I walked over to the computer and started watching..."
"Oh Damn!"

Chapter 7

"Sam?"

"Yes Bazil?"

"Staff meeting in one hour…" Bazil said before he hung up…

"Oh shit!" Sam said out loud as he called Sheila…

"Yes Sam?"

"Staff meeting in one hour…"

"Uh oh…" she said out loud…

"What's wrong Mrs. Henley?" A'Licia asked…

"Staff meeting in one hour…"

"Is that bad?"

"Usually we get more than an hour's notice…" Sheila said as she went down the hall to alert more staff…

"Babe – staff meeting in one hour…" Sam said as he hurried into Joselyn's office…

"What happened?"

"I gotta go – I'll see you in the conference room…" Sam said as he went down the hall to alert more staff…

"Cheryl?"

"Yes Mrs. Osgood?"

"Staff meeting in one hour..." I said as I left before she could ask me any questions...

"Oh my God – what happened?" another employee asked...

"We're about to find out..." Cheryl sighed...

"Are you ready for this?" Bazil asked...

"Yea..." I sighed...

"I wish it was happening tomorrow..."

"So do I..." I breathed as we sat down on the sofa and started kissing...

"Where would you like to go on our honeymoon?"

"Somewhere warm... and tropical..."

"Jamaica..."

"That sounds nice..."

"Trinidad..."

"That sounds nice too..."

"Paradise Island..."

"Ooohhh..."

"You like that?"

"Yeesss..."

"Paradise Island..." Bazil said as he pulled me down on top of him and held me...

"I have so much to do..." I sighed...

"All you need to do is show up and say I do..."

"I can't wait to write about this..."

"When you write... do you write about the sex?"

"Oh yea..."

"Do you feel it all over again?"

"Mmmm Hmmm..."

"Do you get wet?"

"Yes..."

"I was just thinking..."

"Uh huh..."

"You write Erotic Fiction..."

"Uh huh..."

"This is actually going to be an autobiography..."

"Uh huh..."

"Are you going to tell them what we did in the judge's chambers?"

"No..."

"So you're not going to tell them everything..."

"I have to leave some things out..."

"Hmmm... interesting..."

"They'll know you got good dick!" I laughed...

"I don't care about that..." he breathed as he started kissing me on my neck...

"Ooohhh... Stop..."

"Is that what you really want?"

"No..."

"That's what I thought..." he said as he ran his hands from my shoulders to the small of my back and kissed me...

"Bazil..."

"Ssshhhh..." he whispered as he kissed me, moving his hands from the small of my back to my ass...

"Mrs. Osgood?"

"Yes Joselyn?"

"We're ready..."

"Thank you Joselyn..." I said as I went to get up and Bazil pulled me back down...

"Bazil..."

"Ssshhh..." he said before he kissed me hard...

"Bazil... they're waiting..."

"So am I..." he breathed...

"Let's do this..." I said as I got up and adjusted myself...

"Okay..." Bazil said as he got up, adjusted himself, took my hand, and we walked to the conference room. Everyone got really quiet as we walked in. We went to the head of the table and Bazil put his arm around me before he spoke... "Thank you all for coming. We called this meeting to make an announcement. Osgood Publishing will be closed for Valentine's Day this year..."

"Woo Hoo!"

"Thank you!"

"Yeeaaa!" Bazil and I waited for everyone to quiet down before he continued...

"My wife and I will be renewing our vows on Valentine's Day at 5pm on the Beach here in Milford..."

"Aww…" everyone said in unison…

"If you wish to attend, please confirm your attendance with Joselyn so we know how many seats we need…"

"I'm going!"

"Me too!"

"You know I'm going!"

"We don't have much time – we have a lot to do – so unless anyone has any questions…

"I have a question…" Shadajah said…

"Yes Shadajah?"

"Can we take pictures?"

"Yes – but there's a catch…"

"What's the catch?"

"We get a copy of all of them…"

"I have a question…" A'Licia said…

"Yes A'Licia?"

"Can we bring anybody?"

"We prefer employees and their significant other's only…"

"Oh good – that means I can bring my husband…"

"Yes – you can bring your husband…"

"If there aren't any other questions – we need to get back to the office…" I said. The room was quiet for a few moments… "Okay – see you all soon…" I said as Bazil took my hand, we left the conference room, and we went to Sheila's office…

"Yes?" Sheila said as we walked in…

"Sheila, did you get a chance to speak with your husband?" I asked...

"I did..."

"Will you be joining us?"

"We will..."

"Oh good!" I sighed...

"C'mon Mrs. Osgood – we have work to do..." Bazil said as he smiled at me mischievously..."

"Yes Mr. Osgood..." I sighed as we went to Joselyn's office...

"I'm already on it..." Joselyn laughed...

"You are?" Bazil asked...

'We got this..." Shadajah said...

"Le'me see..." I said as I sat down next to Joselyn...

"Mr. Osgood – pull up a chair..." Joselyn laughed. Bazil pulled up a chair and sat down next to me as we looked on the computer. We looked around and we thought this was the best one..." Joselyn said...

"Hmmm... Gulf Beach Weddings..." Bazil said...

"We thought this was good because you're renewing your vows – the other places want to give you a wedding and a reception..." Shadajah said...

"They have packages that are really nice – from small to large – we were thinking since you invited the employees you might want the Wedding Dreams package – all the packages include a photographer and music – but you can upgrade to a Gazebo and you get up to 30 chairs..." Joselyn said as she showed us the package...

"Ooohhh... this is Beautiful..." I said...

"It's nice..." Bazil agreed...

"They also gave you vows – I think that's nice because we can all say something different..." Joselyn said...

"I like that..." I said...

"The Perfect Package comes with the Gazebo, a photographer, music, and chairs for up to 50 guests..." Shadajah said as she showed us the package...

"Ooohhh... I like this one too!" I exclaimed...

"So do I..." Bazil said...

'This package also gives you an option to add Rose Petals..." Shadajah said...

"Aww..." I said...

"The Celebration Package includes a photographer, 1 hour video service on DVD, 1 hour live music, a Rose Petal Aisle Way, and chairs for up to 100 guests... and you also get the Arch or the Gazebo..." Joselyn said as she showed us the package...

"I want this one!" I squealed...

"Me too..." Bazil said...

"Me too!" Joselyn and Shadajah said in unison and then we all bust out laughing...

"What vows do you want?" Joselyn asked...

"Well – since we're renewing our vows – I like the Commitment Vows..."

"Okay – they have a wedding officiant for the ceremony, and..."

"Joselyn?" I interrupted...

"Yes Mrs. Osgood?"

"Judge Duffey is going to perform the renewal of our vows and his wife is going to witness..."

"Oh..."

"What's wrong?"

"Nothing – I'ma talk to Sam..." Joselyn said as she jumped up out her chair and hurried out...

"We'll see you later Shadajah – c'mon Bazil..." I sighed as I got up to leave and Bazil followed...

"Sam – we have a problem..." Joselyn said...

"What's wrong Babe?'

"They want Judge Duffey to renew our vows..."

"Oh..."

"I don't want to renew our vows with Judge Duffey!"

"I'm not crazy about the idea either, but I can do it..."

"How can you do it after the way Mrs. Osgood was treated in the court room?"

"After everything she went through, she wants that man to renew their vows – if they can do it, I can do it..."

"I dunno Sam..." Joselyn sighed as Sheila walked in...

"What's wrong?" she asked...

"Mrs. Osgood told me Judge Duffey is renewing our vows and his wife is going to witness..."

"Oh no! I don't want that!" Sheila exclaimed...

"I don't either..." Joselyn sighed...

"Let's go tell them..." Sheila said as they all headed down to our office...

"Bazil?"

"Yes Sam?"

"Can we come in?"

"Who's we?"

"Me, Joselyn, and Sheila..."

"Sure – come in..."

"We need to talk to you..." Sheila said...

"Is something wrong?"

"We don't want Judge Duffey for our vow renewal..." Sheila said...

"Sam?"

"Yes Bazil?"

"How do you feel about it?"

"To be honest – I'm surprised you want it – but if you want it, I'm okay with it..."

"Joselyn?"

"Yes Mr. Osgood?"

"How do you feel about it?"

"I don't want it – can't we use the wedding officiant from Gulf Beach?"

"My wife wants Judge Duffey..." Bazil said as he got up... "Sam – we'll be leaving for the day..." Bazil said as he took my hand, we walked past them, and left the building.

Chapter 8

"Let's go to Bridge House..." I said after we got in the car...

"As you wish..." Bazil said as he picked up my hand, kissed it, and drove out the parking lot...

"Damn..." Sam said...

"Is he really mad?" Joselyn asked...

"Yea..."

"Well what were we supposed to do – renew our vows and act like we don't remember what happened in the court room?" Sheila asked...

"That's exactly what we were supposed to do..." Sam sighed...

"Welcome to Bridge House Mr. Osgood, Mrs. Osgood – how are you?" the waitress asked...

"We're good – thank you for asking..." Bazil said...

"What can I get you to drink?"

"I'll have a glass of merlot..." I said...

"I'll have one too..." Bazil said...

"I'll be right back with your drinks..." the waitress said as she went to get our drinks...

"I don't think this is a good idea..." I sighed...

"I do..."

"You do?"

"I do..."

"First Keisha, now Sheila, Sam, Joselyn..."

"I know – and I'm disappointed..."

"I'm sorry – we should 'a just renewed our vows in the court house..."

"No we shouldn't – I agree with Keisha – that's not romantic..."

"I was really looking forward to the wedding on the beach..."

"We can still do that, and we're going to have Judge Duffey too..." Bazil said as he kissed me...

"I love you..."

"I love you too..."

"Here's your drinks..." the waitress said as she put our glasses of wine on the table... "Are you ready to order?"

"I'll have the BH Burger..." Bazil said...

"Me too..." I said...

"Well done?"

"Well done..." we both answered in unison...

"Okay – I'll be back..." she said as she walked away...

"I just wanted everyone to be happy on Valentine's Day..." I sighed...

"You know what?"

"What?"

"We're not responsible for anybody's happiness but ours..."

"I know – but..." Bazil pulled me into a kiss and kissed me hard...

"Mmmm... I love when you do that..." I breathed...

"Here's what's going to happen..."

"Okay..."

"We're going to renew our vows on the beach..."

"Okay..."

"Judge Duffey will perform the ceremony..."

"Okay..."

"His wife will witness..."

"Okay..."

"It's going to be me, you, Troy, Keisha, Smalls, and Josefina..."

"You don't want Sam, Joselyn, Sheila, or Henley?"

"They don't want it..." Bazil answered as we finished our wine...

"Here's your burgers..." the waitress said as she put our plates on the table...

"This looks really good..." I said as I picked up the burger and took a bite..."

"Would you like another glass of wine?" the waitress asked...

"Yes please..." I answered...

"And you?" she asked Bazil...

"Mmmm Hmmm..." He acknowledged as he took a bite of his burger. The waitress went to get our wine and we finished eating our burgers and fries...

"Would you like to see a dessert menu?" the waitress asked as she put our glasses of wine on the table...

"I'd love too – I don't have room for dessert – but I'd love to see it..." I laughed...

"I'll bring you the dessert menu... and I'll bring you the check..." she laughed as she went to get both...

"I wish tomorrow was Valentine's Day..." I sighed...

"It is..." Bazil breathed as he kissed me...

"Here's the dessert menu, and here's your check..." the waitress said as she placed them on the table...

"Thank you..." Bazil said...

"You're welcome – always nice to see you..." she said as we got up, paid the check, and left...

"Hey y'all – we need to talk to you..." Keisha said as soon as she saw us..."

"Not you too..." I sighed...

"What? What happened?'

"C'mon in..." Bazil said as he opened the door and we all went inside...

"Aww shit – this nice!" Keisha said as she went into the library and threw herself back on the sofa...

"Okay!" Troy said as he went into the library, went over to Keisha, and lay on top of her...

"Let me up Troy..."

"No..." he laughed...

"I'ma tickle you..."

"So..." Keisha started tickling Troy and Troy laughed...

"I'on care... haa... haa... you can... tickle... me... all... you... want... haa... haa..."

"You gon' get up?"

"Nope... haa... haa..."

"You gon' get up eventually..." she sighed...

"Gimmie a kiss..."

"Nope..."

"I said Gimmie a kiss!" Troy growled in her neck...

"Troy... stop... haa... haa..."

"Gimmie a kiss..."

"Okay..." Keisha sighed and then they started kissing...

"Ummm... we'll be in the living room..." Bazil laughed and then we went to the living room and sat down...

"You think they're gonna come back and get us?" Keisha asked...

"Nope..." Troy laughed...

"We should lock the door on they ass!"

"Okay..." Troy said as he got up, turned to go towards the door, and Keisha jumped up off the sofa and ran out the library...

"Told you you was gonna get up!" she laughed as she hurried into the living room and sat down with us...

"I'ma remember that when we get home..." Troy said as he came into the living room and sat down beside Keisha...

"What do you want to talk to us about?" I asked...

"We wanna know if we can wear what we want..." Keisha said...

"Well – we're wearing what we got married in in Vegas..." I said...

"Is it okay if we wear something else?"

"You can wear whatever you want..." Bazil said...

"What kind of vows do you do for a renewal?"

"Joselyn picked a nice package for us from Gulf Beach – they have a few vows to choose from, so I chose Commitment because we're still committed to each other..." I answered...

"Oh that's what's up – I like that!" Troy exclaimed...

"So you're still gonna renew your vows with us?" I asked...

"Yea..." Keisha sighed as she pulled Troy into a kiss... "What happened Beautiee?"

"Joselyn and Shadajah showed us packages from Gulf Beach – but wait – before that we had a staff meeting and we announced that we would be closed for Valentine's Day because we were renewing our vows at Milford Beach..."

"Oh wow! They get the day off? With pay?" Troy asked...

"Yes..." Bazil answered...

"Damn – you got any positions open?"

"If you're serious, I'll look into it..."

"Troy ain't serious – go 'head Beautiee..." Keisha said...

"Well – we picked the package we wanted and we went back to our office..."

"Beautiee was so happy..." Bazil said...

"So we weren't even in our office five minutes and Sam, Joselyn, and Sheila came in to tell us they don't want to renew their vows with Judge Duffey..." I sighed...

"So wait a minute – you closed the office – paid them for the day, invited them to renew their vows with you – and they don't wanna do it because it's Judge Duffey?"

"Yea..."

"I just didn't wanna do it in the court house because I don't think the courthouse is romantic – but I'on care if it's Judge Duffey..."

"Me either..." Troy said...

"Well – it will be me, Beautiee, you, Troy, Smalls, and his wife..." Bazil said...

"Oh shit! You're uninviting them?" Troy asked...

"They're still invited – they just won't be renewing their vows with us..."

"Damn – I'm sorry y'all..." Keisha said...

"So am I – and I'm disappointed – my wife doesn't ask for much – but whatever she asks for I'm going to make sure she gets it..." Bazil said as he pulled me into a kiss...

"I love you..."

"I love you too..."

"I love y'all... Keisha said...

"C'mon Keisha – let's give them some time..." Troy said as he got up...

"See you later..." I said as I got up to hug them...

"See you later..." Bazil said as he got up to hug them too...

"Ummm... I love y'all – but we can't leave if you don't let us go..." Keisha laughed...

"Okay, okay..." Bazil laughed as we all walked to the foyer and then they left...

"You still waiting?" I asked...

"Yes... yes I am..."

"You wanna go swimming?"

"Yes... yes I do..." he said as we undressed on our way out to the pool.

Chapter 9

"Don't be walkin' up in here like I didn't sleep with you last night..." Henley laughed as he pulled Sheila into a hug...

"I'm sorry..." Sheila said as she put her arms around Henley's neck and kissed him...

"How was work?"

"It was interesting..." she answered as she went into the kitchen and sat down at the table...

"I'll make us some tea..." Henley said as he took two cups out the cabinet, took the herbal tea out the cabinet, placed everything on the counter, turned on the tea kettle, and sat down at the table with Sheila... "What happened?"

"Well – they called a staff meeting..."

"About what?"

"About their wedding..."

"Okay..."

"They are closing the company on Valentine's Day because they are renewing their vows..."

"Y'all gettin' paid for the day?"

"Yes – anytime they close the company, we get paid..."

"Okay!"

"Employees and their significant others are invited..."

"That's nice – so what's so interesting?"

"Well – Judge Duffey is performing the vow renewals..."

"The judge she was in court with?"

"Yes..."

"You're right – that is interesting..."

"Well – we told them we didn't want to renew our vows with Judge Duffey..."

"Sheila! Why would you do that?"

"Because we remember what happened to her in court and we don't like him..."

"He let her go didn't he? He didn't have to set the verdict aside – he could 'a locked her up – you don't have to like him – I like him!"

"You weren't even there!" Sheila laughed...

"I don't need to be in court when a white judge let's a black man – or a black woman – go free – especially after they were found guilty!"

"I never thought of it like that..."

"I betcha she did – that's why she asked him to do it – she could 'a asked anybody else to do it – but she didn't..." Henley said as the kettle went off and he got up and made them both a cup of tea. Sheila sat there thinking while Henley was making the tea. Henley put the cups of tea on the table, sat down, and took Sheila's hand... "Didn't you tell me Mrs. Osgood promoted Joselyn the first day she got there?"

"Yes..."

"And Joselyn told her she was tired so they hired two interns and made her a supervisor?"

"Yes..."

"So she did that for Joselyn, you got a new intern, and you get invited to renew your vows with them – on the beach – you get invited to dinner, you get paid for the day – and you don't want to do it because you don't like the judge?"

"Joselyn doesn't like the judge either..."

"Yea? Well she's wrong too..." Henley said as he picked up his tea, got up from the table, went into the living room, and turned on the game...

"We messed up..." Joselyn said as they walked inside...

"You messed up..." Sam laughed...

"I guess I did..." Joselyn sighed...

"See – it doesn't matter to me one way or the other – I don't have to like Judge Duffey – 'cause I love them..."

"I saw Bazil's face..."

"I saw his face too – and I know what it means..."

"What does it mean?"

"He's disappointed..."

"I don't wanna go back to work tomorrow..."

"We have to – and I have to talk to him..."

"You're gonna apologize?"

"I'm gonna tell him we'll do it..."

"Sam!"

"Babe – I love you – hear me out..."

"Okay..." she sighed...

"Beautiee promoted you on her first day there..."

"Yea... she did..."

"Beautiee hired two interns so you wouldn't have to work so hard – and she didn't demote you..."

"Yea... you right..."

"We started going to lunch again – I missed that..."

"Me too..."

"We get to renew our vows on the beach, we get to go out to dinner, and we get paid for the day..."

"I probably hurt her feelings..." she sighed...

"I'll fix it tomorrow..." Sam said as he pulled Joselyn into a kiss...

"I love you..."

"I love you too..."

Chapter 10

"Good morning Mother..." Joselyn said as Sheila came into her office...

"Good morning..." Sheila sighed...

"What's wrong?"

"I told your father we didn't want Judge Duffey renewing our vows – and ooohhh chile..."

"Mommy! What happened?"

"He gave me a good talkin' to and then he got up and left me sitting at the table..."

"No he didn't!"

"He most certainly did..."

"Well – you not the only one..." Joselyn sighed...

"Sam gave you a good talkin' to too?!"

"He did..."

"I'm going to apologize to Mr. Osgood as soon as he comes in..."

"I'ma let Sam talk to him..."

"Your father reminded me of a lot of things..."

"Sam did the same thing..."

"You know they're right – right?"

"Yes Mother!" Joselyn laughed...

"Good morning Bazil – can I speak to you?" Sam asked...

"Of course..." Bazil answered as Sam went into the office and closed the door behind him...

"Look – I just wanted to say we'd be happy to renew our vows with you – if you'll still have us..."

"Really? How does your wife feel about that?"

"She's okay with it..."

"I'll talk to my wife and let you know..."

"Okay..." Sam said as he got up to leave..."

"Oh – before I forget – I need you to let me know if the numbers make sense for us to hire another Vice President..."

"Am I fired?"

"Fired? Aaaaa Haaa.... Aaaaa Haaa..." Bazil laughed... "What in the world would make you think – you know what – never mind..." Bazil laughed again...

"Well – you did say you wanted to hire another Vice President..."

"Yes Sam – I said hire another one – not a new one..."

"Okay..."

"Sam – we started together – and we're going to finish together – I couldn't run this company without you – you have a job for life..."

"Dammit Bazil!" Sam exclaimed as he started tearing up...

"I love you too..." Bazil said...

"I'ma go now..." Bazil said as he left and went to see Joselyn...

"Oh my God! Sam!"

"I'm alright..." he said as he wiped his eyes...

"You sure?"

"I'm sure..."

"Did you talk to Bazil?"

"I did..."

"What'd he say?"

"He said he'll talk to his wife and let us know..."

"Good morning Mr. Osgood – may I speak with you?" Sheila asked...

"Of course..." Bazil answered as Sheila went into the office and closed the door behind her...

"I wanted to apologize for the way I came in here yesterday..."

"Apology accepted..."

"I spoke to my husband last night and he reminded me of a few things..."

"Did he?"

"Yes he did..."

"So what are you saying?"

"I'm saying if you still want us to renew our vows with you, we'll do it..."

"I'll speak to my wife and let you know..."

"Okay..." Sheila said as she got up and left the office...

"There you are..." Bazil said as I walked in with two cups of coffee... "Let me get that..." Bazil said as he got up, took the coffee from me, and placed the cups on his desk...

"What are you working on?" he asked as I sat down behind my desk and took a cup of coffee...

"I'm waiting for some last-minute edits to my cover..."

"You picked out a cover already?"

"Yea..." I sighed...

"Mind if I take a look?"

"I don't mind..." I said as I turned my screen a bit so he could see it...

"I like it..."

"You do?"

"Very much..."

"What do you think of the title?"

"Is that how you see me?"

"Yes – especially when it comes to me..."

"Damn right..."

"I'm not revealing it yet..."

"Why not?"

"I'm going to wait until I finish writing our story..."

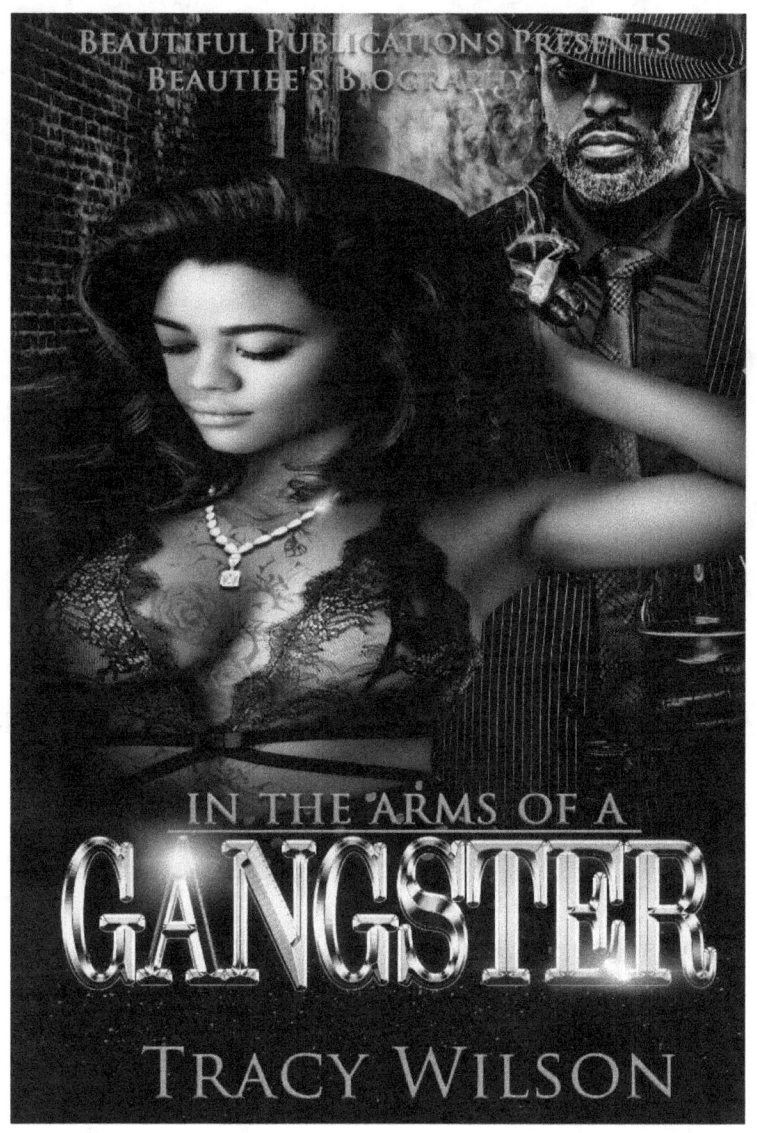

"Mrs. Osgood – May I came in?" Joselyn asked...

"Sure Joselyn – come in on in..." I said as I hurried up and closed my laptop...

"Good morning..." she said as she came in...

"Good morning..." Bazil acknowledged...

"We have 20 people that confirmed for the vow renewals..."

"Oh okay – let's get 50 chairs – this way we'll have a few extra seats – and Joselyn?"

"Yes Mrs. Osgood?"

"Make sure 10 seats are reserved on the right side of Judge Duffey and his wife..."

"Ten seats?"

"Yes Joselyn – 5 couples – me, Bazil, Keisha, Troy, Josefina, Smalls, you, Sam, your mother, and your father..."

"Yes Mrs. Osgood..."

"When we renew our vows, we'll all line up under the Gazebo – Bazil and I will be first in line, then Troy & Keisha, then Smalls & Josefina, then you & Sam, then your mother & father. Bazil and I will go first, and as we all renew our vows, we'll take a seat to the right – unless Bazil has anything he wants to add..."

"I'm fine with it..." Bazil said...

"This package includes live music – I want the first song to be So Nice To Be With You – Smokey Robinson – after that, it doesn't matter what they play because we'll only be outside for an hour – and then we're going to the restaurant for dinner with Judge Duffey and his wife…"

"We're having dinner with the Judge and his wife?"

"Yes we are…"

"That sounds nice…" Joselyn said as she smiled a little…

"When he found out we wanted him to renew our vows, he said he was humbled and honored…"

"Oh wow…"

"I can't wait – I'm so excited – I wish Valentine's Day was tomorrow…" I sighed…

"I'm glad you're happy…"

"I'm glad you're happy too Joselyn…"

"Well – I better get back to my office – oh – before I forget – can we wear whatever we want?"

"Yes Joselyn…" Bazil answered…

"Okay – I need to get back to my office – I have to get this finalized – bye…" Joselyn said as she left and we bust out laughing…

"I love you…" Bazil laughed…

"I love you too…" I laughed…

"I might as well tell you now…"

"Tell me what?"

"Sam came in here to talk to me…"

"He did?"

"Yes – he wanted me to know they would renew their vows if we would still have them…" he laughed…

"What did you say?"

"I told them I'd talk to you and let them know!" he laughed…

"I guess they know now!" I laughed…

"Sheila came in to talk to me too…" he laughed…

"What'd she say?"

"She wanted to apologize…"

"Well that was nice – did you accept her apology?"

"I did…"

"Good…"

"She said her husband reminded her of a few things…"

"Really?"

"Yes…"

"I wonder what he said."

"She didn't tell me…"

"Well – whatever he said – she came in here to apologize…"

"Bazil?"

"Yes Sam?"

"Can I come in?"

"Sure Sam – come in…"

"Good morning Mrs. Osgood…"

"Good morning Sam…" I acknowledged…

"Bazil – I ran the numbers you requested…" Sam said as he placed a folder on Bazil's desk…

"Thank you Sam…"

"You're welcome…" Sam said as he left the office…

"What's that?" I asked...

"I asked Sam to run the numbers for me to see if I could hire a 2nd Vice President..."

"You wanna replace Sam?"

"No – I want to hire a 2nd Vice President – I do not want to replace Sam!" Bazil laughed...

"Okay, okay..." I laughed...

"I asked Sam to run the numbers to see if we could hire a 2nd Vice President so I could offer Troy a job..."

"Keisha said he wasn't serious..."

"Keisha's not the one that asked..."

"You're right..."

"After looking at these numbers, it looks like I can't do it right now..."

"You can't?"

"I could – if I paid him at the low end – but he deserves more..."

"What's the low end?"

"The low end is $135k – the high is $201k..."

"Wow!"

"I want to be able to at least pay him the median – and I can't do that right now..." Bazil sighed...

"Aww... don't feel bad..." I said as I got up, went over to him, and have him a hug...

"I just hope they're okay and he doesn't really need a job..." Bazil sighed...

"If he really needs a job, he'll ask you again – and he'll let you know he's serious..."

"I know…"

"If he does, just find him a job or create a job where the median is $135k – if he really needs a job, he'll be grateful…"

"You're right…"

"Good – now I'm gonna get back to my book before you take me to lunch…"

"Beautiee…"

"Yes Bazil?"

"Don't say anything to Keisha…"

"Okay…."

"Yes Smalls…" Bazil said as he answered his cell…"

"I'm good – thanks for asking…" Smalls laughed…

"Sorry 'bout that – good morning, how are you?"

"That's better – listen – I got a call from Judge Duffey…"

"Uh oh…"

"Everything's fine – he just needs the names of all the couples…"

"Bazil Osgood, Beautiee Osgood…"

"I know those names…" Smalls laughed… "Give me the other names…"

"Jackie Smalls, Josefina Smalls…"

"Oh you got jokes!" Smalls laughed…

"Troy Cochran, Keisha Cochran, Samuel Logan, Joselyn Logan, Sheila Henley, and Thomas Henley…"

"Okay – thanks…"

"Wait!"

"Yea Bazil?"

"Why'd you need all the names?"

"I gotta go…" Smalls said and then he abruptly hung up…

"How's Smalls?" I asked…

"He just hung up on me…" Bazil laughed…

"He's busy – don't take it personal…" I said and then I went back to writing.

Valentine's Day, February 14th, 2020

"Fuck me…" I moaned louder than I usually do…

"Beautiee…" Bazil moaned…

"Bazil… I'm Cummmmiiiinnnngggg! Aaaahhhh!" I screamed…

"Beautiee… Fuck… UUUUGGGGHHHH!" Bazil growled so loud it startled me…

"Wow…" I breathed as I continued riding his dick…

"Yeeessss…"

"I don't know what's gotten into me…" I breathed as he held me by my waist and continued thrusting inside me…

"Meee…" Bazil breathed…

"Yesss…" I breathed as I lay down on him and we started kissing…

"We're getting married… again…"

"Mmmm hmmm…"

"We need to get ready…"

"Mmmm hmmm" Bazil turned me over on my back and now he was on top of me…

"I know you want more…" he breathed as he kissed me…

"Mmmm hmmm…"

"But if I don't get up now... I might not get up at all..."

"Okay..." I sighed and then I pulled him into another kiss...

"Beautiee..."

"I know, I know..."

"Let's go downstairs..." he said as he got up, put on his robe, and held one open for me. I got up put my arms into the sleeves, and Bazil wrapped the robe around me, pulled me to him, and held me...

"I love you so much..." I whispered as I started crying...

"Uh uh..." Bazil said as he kissed my tears..."

"I'm just happy..."

"That's better..." he said as he kissed me again and then we went downstairs to the kitchen... "I'll make coffee..."

"Okay..."

"You still want to go with the Commitment Vows?"

"Yes..."

"Okay..."

"I was just thinking..."

"About what?"

"About how good you looked on our wedding day..."

"Oh yea?"

"When I saw you, I wanted to run to you, rip your clothes off, and fuck you right there..."

"That would've been an interesting video..." Bazil laughed...

"I love you..." Troy breathed as he kissed Keisha...

"I love you too..."

"You ready to do this?"

"Yea..."

"I'd marry you every day if I could..."

"Troy..." Keisha whispered as she started crying...

"I love you... I love you... I love you..." he said as he smothered her with kisses...

"I love you too..." she said through tear-soaked eyes...

"C'mon – I'll make us breakfast..." Troy said as he got up out of bed and put on his boxers..."

"I'm coming..." Keisha said as she got up, put on her robe, and then they went downstairs to the kitchen... "You still wanna go with the Commitment Vows?"

"I don't care what vows we go with – at the end of the day, I'ma still be your wife..."

"I know that's right..." Troy said as he pulled her into a kiss...

"My Fina..." Smalls said as he kissed her...

"Sí mi esposo, mi amor ... Yes my husband, my love..." she breathed as she kissed him back...

"Gracias por amarme... Thank you for loving me..."

"Mi amor... My love" she breathed as she kissed him... "Traté de dejar de amarte ... y no pude ... I tried to stop loving you... and I couldn't..."

"Gracias a Dios no podías dejar de amarme ... Thank God you couldn't stop loving me..."

"Mi amor ... por favor, perdóname por haber pensado que podría vivir sin ti ... My love... please forgive me for ever thinking I could live without you..."

"Te perdono ... te amo ... I forgive you... I love you..."

"Te amaré por siempre... I will love you forever..."

"Mi final ... My Fina..." Smalls whispered as he started crying...

"Por favor no llores mi amor ... Please don't cry my love..."

"Estoy llorando lágrimas de alegría ... I'm crying tears of joy..."

"Te prometo que habrá más alegría ... I promise you there will be more joy..." she said as Smalls pulled her to him, kissed her hard, and they began making love..."

"I don't care what they think about me and..." Sam sang as he stood in front of the mirror shaving...

"I don't care what they say..." Joselyn sang as she startled Sam and he turned around...

"I don't care what they think if you're leaving... 'cause you ain't goin' nowhere..." Sam sang as he pulled Joselyn into a hug and kissed her...

"Ummm... those are not the words..." Joselyn laughed...

"Those are our words..." Sam breathed as he kissed her... to our song..."

"Oh Sam..." Joselyn sighed as they started kissing...

"Sheila!" Henley called out from the bathroom as he shaved...

"I'm in the kitchen!" she yelled back...

"Sheila!" Henley called out again...

"I'm in the kitchen!" she yelled back a little louder...

"Sheila!" Henley called out again...

"Let me go see what he wants now..." Sheila sighed as she got up and went into the bathroom...

"Yes Henley?"

"That's more like it..." he said as he pulled her close to him, held her, and kissed her deeply...

"Oh my goodness..." she breathed... "Is that what you wanted?"

"That's what I wanted..."

"Is that all you want?" she asked as she smiled at him mischievously...

"Now see – you startin' trouble – you know what happens when you start trouble - right?"

"I sure do..." she answered as she took him by the hand and led him into the bedroom...

When we got to the beach we were in awe. The sun was going down and the orange and blue sunset was the perfect back drop for the ceremony. The waves were cascading slowly up to the sand and I could see the photographer and videographer taking pictures and videos. Unbeknownst to us, we were the last to arrive. There were 25 seats to the left filled with employees, their significant others, and a few people we didn't know who took advantage of the opportunity to witness our ceremony. There were also 25 chairs to the right, and the last 15 chairs were filled with more employees. The chairs were white with red ribbons tied to each back leg, and the rose petals were scattered up the walkway to the Gazebo which was also lined with roses. All our friends were on the walkway with the men on the left and the women on the right. Everyone applauded, whistled, and cheered when we started to walk up the walkway and we both started crying. We both took turns hugging Henley, Sheila, Sam, Joselyn, Smalls, Josefina, Troy, and Keisha so it took a bit longer to make it up the walkway to the front of the line but when we finally got there, Judge Duffey handed us tissues, and his wife held a basket with used tissues inside...

"Please put your tissues in here after you finish using them..." she said. Bazil and I did as she asked and then she spoke again... "This basket holds tears of joy from everyone here..."

"Bazil..." I whispered as we started crying again and he pulled me into a kiss...

"My name is Harland Duffey, and this is my wife, Helen. It's been a while since my wife and I have been able to officiate a wedding – especially on Valentine's Day. Each time we do this, we marry the couples that come before us, and we marry each other. We're going to do that again this evening, times five." Judge Duffey waited for everyone to stop applauding, whistling, and cheering before he continued. He came from behind the podium with five bottles of blue sand and his wife came from behind the podium with five bottles of pink sand. Judge Duffey gave each groom a bottle and his wife gave each bride a bottle, and then he went and stood back behind the podium... "I want each couple to come to the Unity Table as I call your name – Bazil & Beautiee..." We went to the Unity Table and his wife put an empty vase on the table...

"You have committed here today to share the rest of your lives with each other. Today, this relationship is symbolized through the pouring of these two individual containers of sand - one representing you Bazil and all that you were, all that you are, and all that you will ever be - the other representing you Beautiee, and all that you were, all that you are, and all that you will ever be. Please pour your sand into the vase..." Bazil and I started pouring our sand into the vase and he continued...

"As these two containers of sand are poured into the third container, the individual containers of sand will no longer exist, but will be joined together as one. Just as these sands can no longer be separated and poured into the individual containers, so will your marriage be." Bazil picked up our vase and we went to the back of the walkway as Troy & Keisha went up to the table, and the Unity of the Sand was repeated with them, Smalls & Josefina, Sam & Joselyn, and finally Henley & Sheila...

"Good evening everyone. Welcome to the celebration of union between Bazil & Beautiee, Troy & Keisha, Jackie & Josefina, Samuel & Joselyn, and Henley & Sheila. Tonight, in front of friends, family, employees, and clients, they honor their commitment to not just gazing at one another, but looking outward together in the same direction. Today, Bazil & Beautiee, Troy & Keisha, Jackie & Josefina, Samuel & Joselyn, and Henley & Sheila, proclaim their love to the

world, and we rejoice with and for them. Bazil &
Beautiee, Troy & Keisha, Jackie & Josefina,
Samuel & Joselyn, and Henley & Sheila, in
presenting yourselves here today you perform a
remarkable act of faith. This faith can grow,
mature, and endure, but only if you are all
determined to make it so. A lasting and growing
love is never automatic, nor guaranteed by any
ceremony. Let the foundation of your union be
the pure love you have for each other, not just at
this moment, but for all the days ahead, honor
faithfully the statements and commitments that
you bring here today. Faults will appear where
now you find contentment, and wonder can be
crushed by the routine of daily living - but today
you resolve that your love will never be blotted
out by the commonplace, obscured by the
ordinary, or compromised by life's difficulties.
Stand fast in that hope and confidence, and
believe in your shared future just as strongly as
you believe in yourselves and in each other today.
Only in this spirit can you create a partnership
that will sustain all the days of your lives. Bazil
& Beautiee, Troy & Keisha, Jackie & Josefina,
Samuel & Joselyn, and Henley & Sheila, we are
here to celebrate as you renew this journey
together. It is in this spirit that you have come
here today to renew these vows.

"Bazil, Troy, Jackie, Samuel, and Henley,
repeat after me to your wives: I take you to be my

partner for life. I promise above all else to live in truth with you and to communicate fully and fearlessly, I give you my hand and my heart as a sanctuary of warmth and peace, and pledge my love, devotion, faith and honor as I join my life to yours."

"Beautiee, Keisha, Josefina, Joselyn, and Sheila repeat after me to your husbands: I take you to be my partner for life. I promise above all else to live in truth with you and to communicate fully and fearlessly. I give you my hand and my heart as a sanctuary of warmth and peace, and pledge my love, devotion, faith and honor as I join my life to yours".

"Bazil & Beautiee, Troy & Keisha, Jackie & Josefina, Samuel & Joselyn, and Henley & Sheila, in so much as you all have agreed to live together in Matrimony, have promised your love for each other by renewing your vows, the joining of your hands, I now declare you all to continue to be husbands and wives."

"By the authority vested in me under the laws of the State of Connecticut, I now pronounce you partners for life. Congratulations - you may kiss."

"I love you Mr. Osgood..."
"I love you Mrs. Osgood..."

"We's married..." Keisha said...

"I know that's right..." Troy said...

"Mi esposo mi amor ... My husband, my love..." Josefina said...

"Mi esposa ... mi para siempre ... My wife, my forever..." Smalls said..."

"I love you Joselyn..."

"I love you too Sam..."

"I still love you Sheila..." Henley laughed...

"I still love you too..." Sheila laughed...

"I present to you Mr. and Mrs. Osgood, Mr. & Mrs. Smalls, Mr. & Mrs. Cochran, Mr. & Mrs. Logan, and Mr. & Mrs. Henley!" Judge Duffey shouted. We all started kissing each other and when So Nice To Be With You started playing we all danced, laughed, hugged, and kissed as each song blended into the next and we didn't realize our time was up until we noticed the staff putting the chairs into the company van...

"Mr. Osgood?" Judge Duffey interrupted as he tapped Bazil on the shoulder...

"Yes your honor..." Bazil answered without looking at him as he held me closer and we continued dancing...

"It's 6:45..."

"Thank you..." Bazil breathed as he pulled me into a deep, passionate kiss... "We better go..." Bazil breathed...

"Okay..." I sighed as we walked along the beach towards the restaurant. When we got up to the entrance, everyone started applauding, whistling, and clapping and we started kissing...

"Congratulations Mr. & Mrs. Osgood – right this way..." the hostess said as we followed her to our table...

"'Bout time y'all got here!" Keisha said as everyone laughed...

"It certainly is..." Bazil said as we sat down on the left side of the table and Judge Duffey and his wife sat down on the right side of the table...

"Good evening..." the waitress greeted... "Congratulations on your vow renewals..."

"Thank you..." we all said in unison...

"May I start you all off with our featured drink, Lousi M. Mautini Caberenet Sauvignon, or would you like something else?"

"We'll have two bottles of Dom Perignon..." Bazil answered...

"Yes Sir – I'll be right back..." she said as she went to get the Champagne...

"Helen, it's so lovely to meet you..." I said...

"Thank you Beautiee – it's lovely meeting you too – it's lovely meeting all of you..." she gushed...

"It's lovely meeting you..." Keisha said...
"Very nice to meet you..." Joselyn said...
"Thank you for witnessing..." Sheila said...
"You're welcome..." Helen said...

"Helen ... eres muy hermosa ... y muy dulce ... Helen... you are very beautiful... and very sweet..." Josefina said...

"Como eres Helen ... como eres ... As are you Josefina... as are you..." Helen said. The waitress came over with a waiter and they placed glasses on the table and poured our champagne as we continued...

"It's really nice to meet you Helen – we hardly ever meet the wife of a Judge..." Henley said...

"That's true – we don't ever meet the wives – this is special..." Sam said...

"Your husband is a lucky man..." Smalls said...

"You remind me of my wife..." Troy said as he smiled at Keisha...

"Helen – thank you for coming, witnessing, and celebrating with us..." Bazil said...

"You're welcome – I couldn't imagine a better Valentine's Day..." Helen said...

"Everyone please raise you glass..." Bazil said as he stood up and went to the front of the table... "Beautiee, please stand beside me..." I stood up beside Bazil and then he continued... "Here's to all of us..."

"To all of us..." we all said in unison as we sipped our champagne...

"When we said we wanted to renew our vows on Valentine's Day, you all could have told us you had other plans, but you didn't – instead,

you chose to be here with us and show us love —
and we'll never forget that..."

"Aww..." everyone said in unison...

"Your Honor, Mrs. Duffey — rather than
spend Valentine's Day alone, you chose to be here
with all of us..." Bazil said as he started to fight
back tears... "My wife was right about you — she
said she wanted you to officiate our ceremony
because you gave us our lives back... and..." Bazil
couldn't finish — he started crying, I started
crying, Judge Duffey was tearing up, and his wife
was crying along with everyone else. Judge
Duffey stood up from the table...

"You're welcome..." he said as he hugged
Bazil and then I pulled Bazil into a kiss before we
sat back down...

"Okay — I'ma need y'all to stop... I can't
take it!" Joselyn said as everyone laughed and
wiped their eyes...

"Uh uh — tissues in the basket!" Helen
exclaimed as she put the basket on the table.
Everyone passed their tissues up to the front of
the table and Helen put the tissues in the
basket...

"Y'all 'bout to run outta room — either we
need another basket — or you women need to stop
cryin'!" Henley said as he dabbed his eyes...

"Oh — look who's dabbing his eyes though!"
Sheila said as we all laughed...

"How's everything here?" the waitress
asked as she came back to the table...

"We'll have four plates of each – Fried Calamari, Crab Cakes, Hot Shot Buffalo Wings, Fried Brussel Sprouts, and Mussels Scampi..." Bazil said...

"Four plates of each – got it!" she said as she went to get our appetizers...

"Oh my goodness – Honey look – they have Seafood Pot Pie!" Helen exclaimed...

"You're kidding!" Judge Duffey said...

"Yes Honey – look!" she said as she showed him the menu...

"We're having the Seafood Pot Pie..." Judge Duffey said...

"I'ma get the Seafood Paella..." Troy said...

"I'ma have the Mango Salmon – that shit sounds good!" Keisha exclaimed...

"I'ma have the Seafood Risotto..." Smalls said

"I'll have the Cajun Grilled Atlantic Cod..." Josefina said...

"I'm getting the Blackened Swordfish Gorgonzola..." Joselyn said...

"I'ma have the Grilled Center Cut Filet Mignon..." Sam said...

"I'ma have the Prime Steak Frites..." Henley said...

"I'll have the Chicken Francaise..." Sheila said...

"I'll have the Chicken Francaise too..." I said...

"I'm going to have the Grilled Center Cut Filet Mignon…" Bazil said as the waitress came back over to the table…

"Looks like you've decided…" the waitress said…

"We have…" Bazil said…

"Okay – I'm ready…"

"Two Grilled Center Cut Filet Mignon, Two Chicken Francaise, Two Seafood Pot Pies, and one of every other entrée on the menu…" Bazil said…

"And two more bottles of champagne…" Judge Duffey said…

"Honey…" Helen started to say…

"Helen – I don't have to work tomorrow – I mean not in the court room – I always have to work in the bedroom…" he laughed…

"Harland!" Helen exclaimed…

"Yes Dear?" Judge Duffey said as he took her hand and kissed it…

"Nothing… I love you…"

"I love you too…"

"Aww…" we all said in unison as the waitress and waiter brought our appetizers to the table…

"Damn this looks good – and I'm hungry!" I exclaimed…"

"Me too…" Sheila said…

"Si, si…" Josefina said as we all started passing the plates and helping ourselves…

"More champagne?" the waitress asked…

"Yes please!" Judge Duffey said...

"Yes Please..." Bazil said...

"None for me..." Smalls said...

"I'll have some more..." Sam said...

"Ummm... Sam?"

"Yes Joselyn?"

"Aren't you driving?"

"Nope..." Sam laughed...

"I'll have another..." Troy said...

"No thank you..." Sheila said...

"None for me..." Joselyn said...

"Here!" Keisha said as we laughed...

"Yes, thank you..." I said...

"I'll have some too..." Helen said...

"How was the food?" the waitress asked...

"I hate Brussel sprouts – but now that I've tasted yours – I like them..." I said...

"I'll be sure to pass that on..." the waitress said... "How was everything else?"

"Good!" we all said in unison...

"That's great – we'll be back with your food in a lil' bit..." she said as she walked away...

"Oh shit! Troy exclaimed when he saw all the food coming...

"Ooohhh... this all looks so good..." I said...

"Who has the Pot Pies?" the waitress asked...

"We do..." Judge Duffey said...

"Okay – who has the Seafood Paella?"

"Me!" Troy said...

"Who has the Mango Salmon?"

"Right here!" Keisha said...

"Who has the Seafood Risotto?"

"Me..." Smalls said...

"Who has the Cajun Grilled Atlantic Cod?"

"Ci, ci..." Josefina said...

"Who has the Blackened Swordfish Gorgonzola?"

"That's mine..." Joselyn said...

"Okay – I have two Grilled Center Cut Filet Mignon..."

"Right here..." Bazil said...

"Right here..." Sam said...

"Who has the Prime Steak Frites?"

"I do..." Henley said...

"Okay – I have two Chicken Francaise..."

"That's for me! I exclaimed..."

"Me too!" Sheila exclaimed...

"Alright! I know you just got your dinner but please feel free to let me know if you want dessert – tonight our dessert is Double Fudge Chocolate Cake..." she said as she walked away...

"Ooohhh.... This looks so good!" Bazil said...

"I'ma 'bout to bust it down!" Troy said... "Right Keisha?"

"Mmmm hmmm..." Keisha said as she ate...

"Oh Honey – this pot pie is delicious..." Helen said...

"Brings back memories..." Judge Duffey said...

"¡Dinos! Tell us!" Josefina said...

"Well..." Helen sighed...

"We had seafood pot pies on our first date..." Judge Duffey said as he took Helen's hand and kissed it...

"Aww..." we all said in unison...

"Is it good Sheila?" I asked...

"Oh yes..." Sheila answered and then she put a piece of chicken in her mouth...

"Damn this shit is good!" Smalls said...

"How's your food Joselyn?" Sheila asked...

"It's delicious..." she sighed...

"You alright Sam?" Bazil asked...

"Oh yea – I'm good!" Sam exclaimed. We finished our food and looked round at each other...

"Who's up for dessert?" Bazil asked...

"I'm always up for dessert..." Judge Duffey said as he smiled at his wife mischievously...

"Harland... what in the world is going on with you?" she asked him...

"It is Valentine's Day..." he answered...

"Yes... it is..."

"Let's get dessert..." Bazil said deliberately... breaking their concentration...

"I don't have room for dessert..." Sheila said...

"Shall I bring the cake?" the waitress asked...

"Yes please..." Bazil answered...

"I don't have room for dessert..." Sheila repeated. When the waitress brought the cake to the table, she changed her mind... "Oh I want some of that!"

"Uh uh – you don't have room for dessert!" Henley said as we all laughed... "I knew when you saw that cake you'd want some..." Henley laughed...

"I feel like singing Happy Birthday..." Keisha laughed...

"I'll leave some plates and the cutter..." the waitress said as she went to get the check..."

"Is she in a hurry?" Joselyn laughed...

"No Joselyn – we're not being rushed – we can stay here as long as we like..." Bazil laughed as he got up, started cutting the cake, and passed down the plates...

"Mmmm... this is good..." Judge Duffey whispered to his wife...

"It's a good thing we don't have to work tomorrow..." Sam said...

"Speak for yourself..." Smalls said...

"You work on Saturdays?" Sam asked...

"I'm an attorney – I work 24-7..."

"Desearía que no trabajaras tan duro ... Te extraño ... I wish you didn't work so hard – I miss you..." Josefina said...

"Sé cómo te sientes Josefina, mi esposo solía trabajar en un tribunal superior, a veces no volvía a casa hasta la medianoche ... I know how you feel Josefina – my husband used to work in a higher court – sometimes he wouldn't come home until midnight..." Helen said...

"That was good..." Keisha said...

"It sure was!" Joselyn and I said in unison and then we all laughed...

"We're ready too..." Judge Duffey said as he stood up and Helen stood up with him...

"Thank you again..." Bazil said...

"You're welcome..."

"Thank you for a lovely evening – it was lovely meeting you all..." Helen said...

"Here..." Judge Duffey said as he handed Bazil $500...

"Oh no..."

"I insist..."

"Yes Your Honor..."

"Good night everybody..." Judge Duffey said as he took his wife by the hand and they left...

"They couldn't wait to leave..." Bazil laughed...

"You peeped them too?" Troy laughed...

"Of course..."

"You ready?" Smalls asked Josefina...

"Listo mi amor ... Ready my love..."

"It's just gettin' past Sheila's bed time..." Henley said...

"We leavin' with them..." Keisha said...

"You ready Joselyn?"

"I'm ready..."

"Okay – let's go home..." Bazil said as we all got up to leave... "I'll see you all outside..." Bazil said as I grabbed the basket and we went to pay the check. When we got outside, everyone was waiting to give us hugs and kisses... "We love you..." Bazil said...

"Love you too!" Henley, Sheila, Joselyn, Sam, Smalls, and Josefina said in unison before they went to their cars. Keisha and Troy walked hand in hand towards the beach and we followed...

"I wish we could stay here a little while..." Keisha sighed...

"We could, but those nice officers are waiting to remind us that the beach is closed..." Bazil said...

"Aiight – let's go..." Troy said as we started walking to the car...

"How was your dinner?" Mike asked as he opened the door for us...

"It was lovely..." Bazil answered as we all got in...

"I'll get you home..." Mike said as he drove off the beach. We got to Keisha and Troy's house first...

"Good night – love y'all..." Keisha said...

"Love y'all..." Troy said...

"We love you too..." Bazil and I said in unison. When we got to our house, Mike got out and opened the doors for us...

"Thank you Mike..." Bazil said...

"Yes Mike – thank you..." I said...

"You're welcome..." Mike said as he got in the car and drove off...

"Are you ready for your wedding night Mrs. Osgood?"

"Yes Mr. Osgood – I'm ready..." I breathed. Bazil opened the door, pulled me inside to the foyer, closed the door, and kissed me hard...

"Oh damn..." I breathed...

"Don't count on getting any sleep tonight..." he said as he picked me up in his arms and carried me upstairs into the bedroom.

Chapter 12

"Bazil? Bazil? Where are you?" I called out... "Hmmm... where the hell is he?" I said as I got up out of bed, put my robe on, and went down stairs... "Bazil? Where are you?"

"I'm in the kitchen..." I walked into the kitchen and smiled when I saw him... "I made coffee..." he said as he put the coffee on the table and sat down...

"Bazil – what's wrong?"

"I changed my mind..." he sighed...

"You changed your mind? What does that mean? You don't want to be married?" I asked as I started tearing up. Bazil got up, came over to me, pulled me up out the chair, and held me...

"Beautiee..." he breathed as he kissed me... "I'm not talking about us..."

"I don't understand..."

"Sit down..."

"Okay..." I sniffed...

"I read your book..."

"Ooohhh..."

"You lied to me..." he whispered as he started crying...

"Bazil... I never lied to you... please don't cry..." I said as I started crying...

"I read what you said about Trevor..."

"I'm sorry..."

"You told me you fucked him to hurt me..."

"I did..."

"You didn't tell me you enjoyed it..." he whispered as he continued crying...

"Bazil... I'm sorry..."

"I knew you fucked him... but when I read all the details..." Bazil couldn't finish... he choked up and started crying hard... and I broke down right along with him...

"I'm sorry!" I cried...

"I know... but... I can't..."

"You can't forgive me?"

"I can't let you publish your book..."

"That isn't fair!" I cried...

"I know... but I can't... Beautiee... please..."

"What if I take it out?"

"You'll do that?"

"I won't remove it completely... but I can take that part out..."

"You're sure?"

"I don't wanna hurt you..." I whispered as I started crying again...

"I'm sorry... I shouldn't've read it..."

"I'm glad you did..."

"You are?"

"Yes..."

"Why?"

"What if you didn't read it and I published it? Everyone would know all the details anyway..."

"You're right..."

"Can I ask you something?"

"Sure..."

"Are you okay... with the library?"

"Yes... and no..."

"I don't understand..."

"When I read it... I realized how much I hurt you... in detail..." he sighed...

"You want me to take that out too?"

"I wish you could take it all out..." he sighed...

"I bet you have no problem reading all about me and Sonia huh?" I snapped...

"That's different..."

"Of course it is..." I sighed as I got up from the table...

"Beautiee... please... sit down..."

"No thank you..." I said as I left the kitchen and started walking towards the library...

"Oh no you don't!" Bazil said as he jumped up from the table, came up behind me, and held me so I couldn't move...

"Let go of me..."

"No..."

"Let go of me..."

"Is that what you want?"

"Yes..."

"Are you sure?"

"Yes..."

"Okay..." he sighed as he let me go and turned to walk away...

"Bazil?"

"Yes Beautiee?"

"Could you make me another cup of coffee?"

"You want me to bring it upstairs?"

"No – I want you to bring it in the library..." I said as I started to walk towards the library and Bazil grabbed me, turned me around, and pulled me into a kiss...

"You know I love you – right?"

"Yes Bazil..." I sighed...

"I'm going to make us both another cup of coffee... and then I'm coming into the library with you..."

"Okay..." I said as I turned to walk towards the library and stopped...

"Aren't you going in the library?"

"I'm going..." I laughed...

"Well?"

"I was waiting to see if you'd grab me again..."

"In that case..." Bazil said as he turned me around and pulled me to him..."

"I love you..."

"I know..." he breathed as he kissed me...

"I'm sorry..."

"I know..."

"Let me go fix it..."

"Okay..." This time I didn't wait – I hurried into the library, sat at my desk, turned on my computer, opened my book, and went straight to the chapter where I fucked Trevor and started reading... "I guess I'll take out chapter 10..." I said as Bazil put the coffee down for me... "Thank you..." I said as I kept reading. Bazil pulled up his chair and sat beside me... "Bazil... no..."

"You want me to move?"

"Yes..."

"Okay..." he sighed as he went back to his desk and pouted. I picked up the coffee, sipped it, and went back to reading. I continued editing, saved it, and looked over at Bazil... "Come read this..." I said. Bazil came over, leaned over my shoulder, and started reading...

"You fucked my husband – I tried to take your fuckin' head off – one good fuck deserves another... and I'm on a mission to collect..."

"Wait... What?"

"I want you to fuck me Trevor..."

"Are you serious?"

"I'm in room 432..." I answered... and then hung up. I poured myself another drink, gulped it down, lay down on the bed, and fell asleep...

"Mmmm.... Bazil... somebody's at the door..." I yawned as I stretched... "Shit – I forgot where the hell I was for a sec..." I said as I got up to answer the door. "Come in Trevor..." I said as I opened the door. Trevor came into the room, closed the door behind him, and walked towards the bar...

"Mind if I pour myself a drink?"

"Help yourself – and pour me another one while you're at it..." I said as I walked over to the bar, took the glass from him, and gulped it down...

"Thirsty huh?" Trever asked as he sipped his drink...

"Finish your drink Trevor..." I demanded as I pulled back the blankets and sheets, sat on the bed, and started undressing myself. Trevor did as he was told, stood up, and started to undress...

I got up out the bed and went to the bathroom. When I came out the bathroom I threw a red towel at him...

"Come back to bed... we have the rest of the night..." he said as he started wiping his crotch...

"No thank you... thanks though..." I said.

"Oh... it's like that?"

"Like what?"

"So... you're finished?"

"Basically..."

"Oh that's fucked up..."

"Ya know – it's a shame you're not straight," I said as I put my put my bag on my shoulder. "You're nice lookin', you have a good job, a nice portfolio, and a nice dick – you could use a refresher course in how to please a woman but overall, I'd say you have potential," I said as I put on my coat and headed towards the door...

"Fuck you Bitch!" he yelled.

"You just did – thanks!" I said as I slammed the door and headed down the corridor towards the elevator...

"Is that better?" I asked. Bazil pulled me up out my chair and kissed me...

"Thank you..."

"You don't have to thank me..."

"Yes I do..."

"So... you're okay with this?"

"I'm okay with it..."

"What about the library? Are you okay with that?"

"Well..."

"What do you need me to change?"

"I wish you could take it all out..." he sighed...

"Bazil..."

"I know, I know..."

"I'll fix it..." I sighed as I sat back down and started reading... "I'll take Daddy out..." I sighed as Bazil smiled... "But I'm leaving everything else in there..."

"What about the condom?"

"What about it? You want me to take that out too?"

"I guess you can leave that in there..." he sighed...

"I think it'll be a good thing..."

"You caught me in the library fucking a man – how's me wearing a condom a good thing?"

"My readers will say thank God he wore a condom..." I answered as I finished editing and finished my coffee...

"Is that it?"

"No..."

"What are you doing now?"

"I'm going out take out some of what happened between me and Sonia..." I answered as I finished editing and finished my coffee... "Bazil?"

"Yes Beautiee?"

"Are you okay with me leaving the part in there about how you met Trevor?"

"I guess..." he sighed...

"What do you want me to change?"

"Could you change some of the details?"

"Sure..." I said as I went back to editing. When I was done, I looked over at Bazil again...

"Come read this..." I said. Bazil pulled his chair over and started reading...

"It's okay Bazil... tell me..." I said as I got up from the table, walked over to him, and put my arm around him...

"I don't want to hurt you Beautiee..."

"I know Bazil... it's okay..."

"One night I was jacking off... he caught me... and one thing led to another..."

"I understand Bazil..."

"How can you understand it Beautiee? I don't even understand it..."

"You're a man... you have needs..."

"It went like that for a while... but..."

"But you caught feelings..."

"Yea... I know I shouldn't have... but I did... I tried not too..."

"You love him don't you?"

"Yes Beautiee..." he whispered with tears in his eyes...

"Why me?"

"I always wanted to get married... like I said... I'm not gay..."

"How does Trevor feel about that?"

"He hates it... but I'll never be that for him... especially now that I have you..."

"Bazil?"

"Yes Beautiee?"

"We're you ever going to tell me about him?"

"Yes Beautiee..."

"What you did was selfish..."

"I know..."

*"You made me love you so I couldn't
leave... even if I wanted to..."*

"I know... I'm sorry..."

*"I know you are... but I have to be
honest..."*

"Yes Beautiee?"

*"I can't lose you," I said with tears in my
eyes..."*

"I love you..." he whispered as he started
crying...

"Please... don't cry..." I whispered as I
kissed him...

"I'm crying because I'm happy..."

"You're happy? I thought..."

"I told you I loved Trevor... and you told
me you couldn't lose me..." he breathed as he
kissed me...

"I can't..."

"I'll never do that to you again..."

"I know..."

"I love you..."

"Hmmm... I think I'm gonna take out what
you did to me in the kitchen..." I said as I turned
towards the computer...

"Leave it..." Bazil said as he started
kissing me on my neck...

"You like that shit!" I laughed...

"Of course..."

"I think I'll take out this part here...." I said as I pointed to the section where I was telling him about the dildo...

"Leave that in there too..."

"Why?"

"Why not?"

"You like that shit too!" I laughed...

"Hell yea!"

"I don't know if I want my readers to know I fucked her with a strap-on..."

"That's the best part!" he laughed. I didn't even look at him... I just kept editing... "You took it out – didn't you?"

"Yes..."

"Did you take out everything?"

"It's still a good read..." I laughed...

"Le'me see..." he said as he leaned over my shoulder and started reading...

"There's something you're not telling me..."

"Yes..."

"Did something happen Beautiee?" he asked as he came over to me and put his arm around me...

"Yea..."

"What happened?"

"Bazil... I never wanted to spend the night... I wanted to go home..."

"Damn..." Bazil laughed as he went to take the bacon out of the pan and start cooking the

omelets... *"You just wanted to bust a nut and bounce..."*

"Yea..."

"I still don't understand why you never spent the night..."

"What does it matter?"

"I'm sorry... I'll stop asking..." he said as he put the bacon and omelets on plates, got forks, brought them to the table and asked again... *"What happened?"*

"I started thinking about you..."

"You did?"

"Yea..."

"That's sweet," he said as he leaned in to kiss me... *"So... you didn't enjoy being with her?"*

"Yes... she made me feel good... and she felt good too..."

"What was it like when you... ate her pussy... did you like it?'

"Yes... I liked it... a lot..."

"I see..." he said as he rubbed his chin in thought...

"She spoke Spanish then too..."

"Damn Beautiee... she thought she was turning you out but you ended up turning her out," he laughed.

"You're right," I laughed. *"She kept asking me if I was sure I've never done it before..."*

"Have you?"

"No Bazil..."

"Beautiee? Beautiee?"

"Oh... sorry... I was just thinking..."
"About what?"
"About Sonia..." I sighed.
"I can't wait to watch you..." Bazil breathed.
"I hope she's willing..."
"She won't give you any trouble..."
"What makes you so sure?"
"She's feeling you... big time..."
"Naaa..."
"Trust me Beautiee... she's feeling you..."
"Okay... if you say so..." I said as I got up from the table and yawned... "I'm going back to bed..."
"I know so..." Bazil said as he followed me back upstairs...

"Yea... it's still a good read..." he said as he pulled me into a kiss...

"Let me save this..." I said as I saved the book and then I logged off... "Now... where were we?"

"Let's move this to the couch..."

"No..." I breathed as I stood up. Bazil watched as I went over to his desk, dropped my robe, jumped up on his desk, lay down on my back, and spread my legs... "Come here..." I breathed. Bazil stood up, came over to the desk, dropped his robe, pulled me down towards the edge of the desk, and eased himself inside me standing up, and started thrusting... "Huh... Huh... Huh... Huh... Huh..."

"Uggh! Uggh! Uggh! Uggh! Uggh!"

"Bazil... Fuck me..."

"Is this what you want?" Bazil growled as he picked up my legs, put them on his shoulders, grabbed me by my waist, and started pounding me...

"Yesss! Fuck me!"

"Uuugh! Uuugh! Uuugh! Uuugh! Uuugh!"

"Bazil... I'm Cummmiiinnng!"

"I'm cumming with you..."

"Aaaaggghhhh!"

"Uuugggghhhh!" Bazil lifted me up off the desk and held me as he slowed down, but continued thrusting...

"Oh my God..." I breathed...

"I know..."

"We can't fuck in the office anymore..." I breathed...

"Why not?"

"I can't be quiet..."

"I told you..." he laughed...

"I can't help it..."

"Neither can I..."

"This desk is better than the one in your office..." I breathed as I wrapped my arms around his neck...

"You want more..." he breathed...

"Yesss..."

"You're ready to cum again..."

"Yesss..."

"Cum for me..." he breathed in my ear as he held me tighter and started thrusting harder...

"Huh... Huh... Huh... Yes... Fuck me... Right there... Don't stop... Aaaaaaggh!"

"Uuugh! Uuugh! Uuugh! Uuugh! Uuuuuuggghhhh!"

"What the hell is wrong with me?" I breathed...

"Nothing..." he breathed as he pulled me into a kiss, lifted me up off the desk, and stood me up...

"I'm hungry..." I breathed...

"You still want more..."

"Always..."

"I'll make us breakfast..." he breathed as he kissed me... and then..."

"We'll go back to bed..." I laughed.

Coffee

"Good morning..." Bazil breathed in my ear as he kissed me awake...

"What time is it?" I moaned as I turned to face him and stretched...

"It's time for us to plan our honeymoon..." he breathed as he kissed me...

"I can't wait..."

"Neither can I..."

"Let's see... I came in Connecticut..."

"I don't understand..."

"I'm counting the places I've had orgasms..." I laughed...

"Oh... I see..." he laughed...

"I came in Connecticut..."

"That's one..." he breathed as he kissed me...

"I came in Las Vegas..."

"That's two..." he breathed as he kissed me again...

"I came in New Jersey..."

"New Jersey?"

"On the plane... remember?"

"That's three..." he breathed as he kissed me again...

"I'm gonna cum in Nassau..."

"That's four..." he breathed as he kissed me again, this time putting his tongue in my mouth...

"Mmmm... where will I cum next?" I breathed...

"Well..." he breathed as he kissed me again...

"You could cum in here..."

"I could..."

"Let's go downstairs..."

"Okay..."

"I'll make us coffee..."

"Okay..."

"I'll make breakfast..."

"Okay..."

"You let me know where you wanna cum..."

"Okay..."

"And I'll make you cum..."

"Okay!" I squealed as I jumped up out the bed, threw on my robe, and ran downstairs to the kitchen...

"I guess you really wanna cum..." Bazil laughed...

"I do!"

"Okay, okay!" he laughed... "Le'me make coffee..." he said as he took out everything he needed. I sat there watching him intently as he added the water to the pot...

"You're making a big pot of coffee..."

"I am..."

"Hmmm... I guess I'll have to wait and see..."

"It won't be long..." he said as the pot started brewing...

"Hmmm... maybe I wanna cum on your desk again..." I sighed...

"Okay..." Bazil acknowledged as he took two cups out of the cabinet, put them on the counter, and went over to the refrigerator...

"Oh – is it cold outside? Maybe I can cum in the pool!"

"Okay..." Bazil acknowledged as he made our coffee, put the cups on the table, sat in the chair, opened his robe, and smiled at me mischievously...

"Oh my goodness..." I sighed as I got up and went over to him... "You have a serious issue that needs to be addressed..."

"I do..." he agreed as he took a sip of his coffee...

"As much as I'd love to sit on your dick right now... I'm afraid that won't be enough..."

"You could start by sitting on my dick..." Bazil said as he pulled me closer...

"Wait here – I'll be right back..." I said as I hurried out of the kitchen. When I came back, I had a pillow from the sofa in the library...

"Beautiee... what..."

"Drink your coffee Bazil..." I commanded as I picked up my coffee, took a few sips, dropped the pillow on the floor, got down on my knees in front of him, and took his dick in my mouth...

"Beautiee..." he moaned. I took my time taking his dick in my mouth all the way down his shaft so he could feel the warmth...

"Mmmm hmmmm..." I hummed on his dick and then I took it out my mouth...

"Damn..."

"Drink some more coffee..." I commanded as I picked up my cup, drank some more, and put it back down on the table. I waited for Bazil to drink some more coffee and put his cup down and then I took his dick in my mouth again...

"Beautiee... Shit..." he breathed as he held my head and started fucking my mouth...

"Uh uh..." I said before I took his dick out my mouth again...

"Beautiee..."

"Finish your coffee..." I commanded as I picked up my cup, finished my coffee, and put the cup down on the table. I watched as Bazil picked up his cup and swallowed the rest of his coffee so fast that he spilled some out his mouth...

"Aww... you spilled some..." I sighed and then I took his dick in my mouth again...

"Fuck!" he breathed as he grabbed my head and fucked my mouth... "That's it... Suck it..." he growled as I relaxed my throat and he hit my

tonsils... "I'm Cummmmiiinnngggg.....
Uuuuugggghhhh!" I swallowed and continued
sucking as Bazil played in my hair... "Beautiee..."
he whispered. I took his dick out my mouth and
looked up at him...

'Yes my Thirst Quencher?"

"Come here..." he said as he helped me up
off my knees. Bazil picked up the pillow; I picked
up our cups, and took them over to the counter...

"Beautiee... what are you doing?"

"I'm getting us some more coffee..." I said
as I smiled at him mischievously. Bazil watched
as I made us coffee and brought it back to the
table...

"I think that's my new favorite way to have
coffee..." he breathed...

"I'm glad you enjoyed it..."

"Have you decided how you want to cum?"

"Not yet..."

"Maybe you should cum the way I did..." he
said as he put the pillow on the floor in front of
me and dropped down on his knees... "Finish your
coffee..." he commanded. I picked up my coffee
and gulped it down as quick as I could, stopping
twice because it was hot... "Spread your legs..." he
commanded as he deliberately took his time
finishing his coffee... "Come here..." he breathed
as he pulled me down in the chair, put my legs on
his shoulders, and dove in...

"Baaazzziiilll!" I moaned as I grabbed his
head and started riding his face...

"Yes Beautiee... that's it..."

"Huh... Huh... Huh..." Bazil started thrusting his tongue inside my pussy and put his nose underneath the hood of my clit...

"Bazil... Haaa... Haaa.... Haaa...." Bazil took his tongue out my pussy, put two fingers in my pussy, and began massaging my G-spot as he continued licking, sucking, and slurping... and my legs trembled.... "Bazil... Haaa... Haaa.... Yes... Yes... Yes... Don't stop... I'm cummmiinnng... I'm cummmiinnng... I'm CUMMMIINNNG! AAAGGGGHHH!" Bazil took his fingers out my pussy but continued licking and sucking softly as I clamped my legs around his head...

"Wow..."

"Wow is right..." I breathed...

"You want more..."

"Yesss..."

"I need to eat first..." he said as he took my legs down off his shoulders, stood up, and helped me up...

"You just ate..." I breathed as he pulled me into a kiss...

"I certainly did..." he breathed.

Chapter 14

"What would you like for breakfast?"

"I'd like a big breakfast..."

"You must be really hungry..." he said as he pulled me into a hug..."

"I am..." I sighed...

"I'll feed you breakfast... and then I'll feed you dessert..." he breathed as he kissed me...

"Okay..." I sighed as I sat down and Bazil went over to the counter. I watched Bazil go in the cabinet and when he took down the box of pancake mix I smiled... "Pancakes..." I sighed...

"Cinnamon pancakes..."

"Ooohhh... that sounds good." Bazil went back in the cabinet, took down the cinnamon, took down the syrup, and started mixing the pancake mix... "I can't wait for us to go on our honeymoon..." I sighed. Bazil smiled to himself as he put the last pancake on the plate and brought the two plates to the table...

"Ooohhh... these smell so good..." I exclaimed as he sat down...

"If you think they smell good..." he said as he put some syrup on the pancakes and cut a piece with a fork... "Wait until you taste them..."

he said as he brought it to my mouth and I tasted
it...

"Oh my God!" I moaned...

"Good?"

"Yeessss...." I breathed...

"Beautiee?"

"Yes Bazil?"

"I want to talk to you about something..."
he said as we started eating...

"Okay..."

"We've been fucking a lot..."

"I know..." I sighed...

"Well... I've noticed..."

"How intense it is?"

"Yes..."

"I love it..."

"So do I... but..."

"Do you want us to stop?"

"Hell no!" he laughed...

"Bazil?"

"Yes Beautiee?"

"Just say it already..." I laughed...

"Are you pregnant?"

"I think so..."

"Why didn't you say anything?"

"I was trying to wait until I could sneak
away and buy a pregnancy test..." I laughed...

"Aww... you wanted to surprise me..."

"Yea..."

"Well.., now that I know what you want to
do... I'll give you some space..."

"Can we plan our honeymoon first?"

"Sure..."

"I wanna wait until after we get back from our honeymoon to take the test..."

"Why?"

"Come here..." I said as I stood up from the table and stood in front of Bazil...

"Yes Beautiee?" Bazil said as he stood up in front of me and pulled me close to him...

"I just want us to get back to where we were before everything happened..." I sighed as I pulled him to me and held him...

"You don't think we're back there yet?"

"We went through so much..."

"I know..."

"We renewed our vows..."

"I know..."

"We're starting over..."

"I know..."

"This is the beginning..."

"The beginning?"

"Yes... the beginning of our life together... again..."

"Beautiee... I don't understand..."

"I'm looking forward to our honeymoon..."

"So am I..."

"I want us to enjoy our honeymoon..."

"So do I..."

"And I want us to have something to look forward to when we get back..."

"Okay..." he sighed and then he pulled me into a kiss...

"I love you..."

"I love you too..."

"Let's go plan our honeymoon..." I said as I let go of Bazil and started to leave the kitchen...

"Let's not..." Bazil breathed as he pulled me back into his arms and kissed me...

"Bazil..."

"We're going to go upstairs..."

"Okay..."

"We're going to take a shower..."

"Okay..."

"We're going to get dressed..."

"Okay..."

"We're going to go to Target..." he breathed and I started laughing... "What's so funny?"

"C'mon..." I laughed as I took his hand and led him into the library..."

"Beautiee..."

"Pull up your chair and sit by me..."

"Okay..." he sighed. Bazil watched me turn on the computer, go to amazon, and order two Clearblue pregnancy tests... and he bust out laughing... "Beautiee – we could've just gone to Target..."

"Yes – we could've gone to Target – we could've gotten caught, and we'd get so caught up you wouldn't let me get any sleep until I took the test..."

"Okay, okay..." he laughed... "When will the tests be delivered?"

"They'll be delivered in two days..."

"So you'll be able to find out if you're pregnant before we go on our honeymoon..."

"Or I can wait until we get back from our honeymoon..." I said as I pulled up the Nassau Paradise Island website...

"It's beautiful..." Bazil whispered...

"I love it too..."

"How are we going to choose?"

"I've narrowed it down..." I answered as I clicked on the British Colonial Hilton...

"This is a nice hotel..."

"I like it too..." I said as I clicked on the suites...

"Lots of windows..."

"I love the view..."

"So do I..." I clicked on the views and Bazil noticed the Leisure Escapes package...

"Click that one..."

"Okay..." I said as I clicked on it...

"Hmmm... they give you a $50 daily credit... we can use that for any of their services..."

"When do you want to leave?"

"Let's leave next week..."

"Okay... how about Wednesday?"

"You wanna spend the weekend?"

"Yea..."

"Let's leave Monday..."

"As in tomorrow?"

"Yes..."

"Bazil... we need more time..."

"Okay – we'll leave on Wednesday – and we'll stay until the following Friday..."

"Okay – we'll check in on Wednesday, the 19th – and we'll check out on Saturday, the 29th..."

"I want the Ocean View 2 Room Suite..."

"I want that one too..." I sighed...

"Book it..." he said as he gave me his Black American Express... and I bust out laughing...

"Do you always carry your credit card in your robe?" I laughed...

"Not always..." he breathed in my ear as he started kissing me on my neck...

"Ooohhh... that feels good..." I breathed as I hurried up and booked the reservation...

"Are you done?" he asked as he continued kissing me on my neck...

"Mmmm... no.... I need to book our flight..." I answered as I went to Expedia.com...

"Hurry up..." he whispered as he reached around on the right and pinched my nipple...

"Bazil... stop it..."

"No..." he breathed as he began nibbling on my earlobe...

"Bazil... that tickles..." I laughed...

"I know..."

"Look..." I said, interrupting what he was doing...

"Okay... what am I looking at?"

"They have two non-stop flights..."

"Pick the 10:07 a.m...." he said and then he started kissing my neck again...

"Bazil..." I laughed... "Look..."

"What am I looking at now?"

"They have two non-stop flights – one at 11:37 a.m. and one at 2:27 p.m. – and they only have 3 seats left on that one..."

"Pick the 2:27 p.m. one..."

"What if we don't sit together?"

"We'll sit together..." he breathed in my ear...

"Okay – I'll select the Economy Flexible..." I breathed as Bazil started moving his hand up my thigh... "I'm done!"

"Good..." he said as he stood up and held out his hand for me to take. I took his hand and stood up... "Where do you want me?"

"In the shower..."

"As you wish..." he said as he took me upstairs, led me into the bedroom, into the bathroom, and into the shower.

Chapter 15

"Who's knocking on the door at 8: a.m.?" Bazil asked as he went to the door... "Who is it?

"UPS..."

"Okay – hold on a minute..." Bazil said as he opened the door...

"Good morning..." the driver said as he handed Bazil a box from amazon and a letter...

"What's this?"

"It was in your mailbox..."

"Thank you..."

"You're welcome – have a great day..." the driver said as he went to get back in the truck and Bazil closed the door...

"Beautiee?"

"Yes Bazil?"

"It's here..."

"Okay..." I said as I hurried downstairs... "Let me have it!" I exclaimed...

"Alright – here!" Bazil laughed as he gave me the box and I ran upstairs with it...

"Oh no you don't!" Bazil exclaimed as he ran upstairs behing me...

"I'm not opening it!" I laughed as I ran into the bedroom, sat on the bed, and ripped the box open...

"I thought you weren't opening it..." he laughed...

"I'm not – I'm going to put these tests in the drawer in the bathroom – and then we're going to the airport...

"You better be glad we're going to the airport..." he said as he pulled me into a kiss... "Otherwise, you'd be in that bathroom taking a pregnancy test..."

"I'll make it up to you..."

"I know..." he said as he pushed me down on the bed..."

"Bazil... we can't..."

"We can..." he breathed as he started unbuttoning my blouse...

"Bazil... stop..."

"Is that what you really want?" he breathed and then he kissed me hard...

"We'll be in Nassau before the end of the day... we'll check in... we'll go to our room... and then we'll fuck as much as you want..."

"You promise?"

"I promise..."

"Okay..." he breathed and then he got up...

"I'm going downstairs..." he said as he left the room...

"Oh thank God!" I said out loud as I jumped up, grabbed the pregnancy tests, ran into the bathroom, threw them in the drawer, and ran downstairs...

"Beautiee..."

"Yes Bazil?"

"Here..." he said as he handed me a letter...

"Harpo Productions – isn't that Oprah's Production Company?"

"Yes..." I started reading the letter...

"Dear Mr. & Mrs. Osgood,

I hope you're doing well. I'll get to the point. I'm writing to request that you give me an opportunity to interview you on my show..."

"Uh uh..." I said as I continued reading...

"Before you say no, please consider the following:

1.   I promise – I won't put you on trial. My viewers are interested – I'm interested – in hearing what you both have to say.

2.   We can stop anytime you want – if I ask you a question you don't want to answer – if you want to stop in the middle of the interview and walk off the stage (I pray you won't of course – but if you do) I'll understand.

3.   *You can invite anybody you want to be guests in my audience.*

I know you've refused to do interviews in the past, but please consider my request.

Sincerely,

Oprah"

"Hmmm..." I sighed...
"What do you think?"
"Well... we're in a better place now..."
"That's true..."
"I don't think Oprah can do anything to us that hasn't been done to us already..."
"That's true too..."
"I've seen her do interviews before – she'll ask tough questions, but she'll treat us with dignity and respect..."
"You think so?"
"Bazil!" I exclaimed...
"What Beautiee?"
"I know why she wants to interview us..."
"You do?"
"She read my book..." I laughed...
"You think so?"
"I know so..."
"You wanna do it?"
"Yea..."
"Beautiee... are you sure about this?"

"I think so..."

"So we're doing this..."

"Yea..."

"Okay – when?"

"We're going on our honeymoon today – let's schedule it for when we get back..."

"So you wanna schedule it for Monday, March 2nd?"

"Yea..."

"Okay – we'll schedule it as soon as we get back..."

"What time is it now?"

"It's 8:30..."

"Let's go to the airport now – I'll respond to her on the plane – oh – one more thing..."

"Yes Beautiee?"

"Can we wait until after we do the interview before I take the pregnancy test?"

"You better be glad I love you..." Bazil said as he pulled me into a kiss...

"I am..." I breathed as I kissed him back. Bazil grabbed his keys, grabbed the luggage, and we headed to the airport.

As soon as we got settled, I pulled out my laptop and responded to Oprah's letter...

"Dear Oprah,

*Thank you for inviting us on your show.
As requested, we read your letter entirely after
we immediately said no - and then we decided to
accept your invitation.*

*My husband and I discussed it and, based
on past interviews I've viewed, we believe we
you'll treat us with dignity and respect. As you
said – we've already been on trial and that is an
experience we'd rather not repeat.*

*We are inviting the following people to be
guests in your audience:*

*Samuel Logan
Joselyn Logan
Sheila Henley
Troy Cochran
Keisha Cochran*

*We are available for an interview on
Monday, March 1st. Please let us know if this is
convenient for you. We look forward to see you.*

Sincerely,

Beautiee"

Chapter 16

"Welcome to the British Colonial..." the hostess said as we were escorted into the hotel....

"Thank you..." we both said in unison as we walked into the lobby...

"Oh wow – it's even more beautiful in person..." Bazil breathed...

"It certainly is..." I agreed...

"May I have your name?" the clerk asked when we got up to the counter...

"Bazil & Beautiee Osgood..."

"Bazil Osgood? As in Osgood Publishing?"

"Yes..."

"Can I get a picture with you? Please?"

"Beautiee? Is that okay?" Bazil asked me...

"As long as I can get in the picture with you..." I answered...

"Of course!" she squealed as she ran out from behind the counter and took a selfie with us...

"Thank you so much!"

"You're welcome..." Bazil said...

"Here's your keys – your suite is on the 3rd floor..." she said as she handed Bazil the keys...

"We'll get your bags up to your room for you..." the hostess said as we began walking up the staircase...

"This is fabulous..." Bazil said...

"It sure is..." I agreed. When we got upstairs and got to our room, Bazil opened the door and I started to walk inside but he stopped me...

"Wait here..."

"Okay." I watched as Bazil took the bags into the room and then he came back out into the hallway and picked me up in his arms, carried me into the room, kicked the door closed, and carried me to the bed and laid me down on it...

"You made me a promise..." he said as he got undressed...

"Yes my Thirst Quencher..." I breathed...

"It's time to keep that promise..." he said as he got on the bed, lay beside me, and began undressing me...

"Yes my Thirst Quencher..." Bazil unbuttoned my blouse, unclasped my bra, removed them both, and alternated between my left and right breast swirling his tongue around my nipples... "Bazil..." I moaned...

"I know..." he breathed as he opened my pants and slid them off me along with my panties... "Bazil..." I moaned again as he kissed his way up my body, spreading my legs as he did so, until he reached my mouth and then he eased himself inside me... "Huh... Huh... Huh..." I moaned in his mouth...

"Mmmph... Mmmph... Mmmph..." Bazil was smothering me with his mouth and his tongue as he started fucking me harder...

"Mmmm! Mmmm! Mmmm! Mmmm!"

"Mmmph! Mmmph! Mmmph! Mmmph!"

"Mmmm! Mmmm! Mmmm! Mmmm!"

"Mmmph! Mmmph! Mmmph! Mmmph!" Bazil was fucking me harder now and I was cumming all over his dick as he was cumming inside me...

"Mmmm!"

"Mmmph!"

"Mmmm!"

"Mmmph!"

"Mmmm!"

"Mmmph!"

"Mmmm!"

"Mmmmmmppphhhh!"

"Mmmmmmmmmmm!"

"Beautiee..." he breathed...

"Yes... my Thirst Quencher..."

"That was intense..." he breathed...

"It sure was..." I breathed...

"Let's just lay here for a while..."

"Okay..." I breathed as we both fell asleep.

"Mmmm... what time is it?" I yawned...

"It's 7 p.m...."

"I'm hungry..."

"So am I..." he breathed as he kissed me...

"Bazil... I need to eat..."

"So do I..." he breathed as he got on top of me and started kissing his way down my body...

"Bazil..."

"Okay... we'll go eat..." he said and then he kissed me... "But after we eat... I want dessert..." he said as he got up and started getting dressed...

"I love dessert..." I said as I smiled at him mischievously...

"If you don't get dressed... I'm taking you back to bed... and I'm not letting you up until tomorrow morning..."

"Okay, okay!" I laughed as I got dressed... "Where are we going?"

"We're going to the Seafire Steakhouse..." Bazil answered as he took my hand and we left the hotel...

"Welcome to Seafire — what can I get you?" the waitress asked...

"I'll have the Steakhouse Burger..." I answered...

"Would you like that well done?"

"Well done..."

"I'll have the same..." Bazil said...

"I'll be back... she said as she left...

"This is a nice restaurant..." I sighed...

"We can come back if you want..."

"Okay..."

"When we finish our burgers, I want to go to the Aura Night Club..."

"Okay..." I sighed as the waitress put two glasses of water on the table...

"Hmmm... I'm surprised she didn't ask what we wanted to drink..." I said...

"We didn't tell her we wanted anything..." Bazil laughed...

"It's fine – I'll drink water now... and liquor when we get to the nightclub..."

"I like when you get drunk..."

"I like it too... as long as you can carry me..." I laughed...

"Here's your burgers – enjoy!" the waitress said as she left the burgers on the table along with the check...

"I guess she's in a hurry..." Bazil laughed as we ate. When we were finished eating, we went over to the Aura Nightclub, which is located in the Atlantis Hotel, on top of the casino. We walked up the grand staircase and when we got to the top, we saw the sunken glass dance floor and we were in awe...

"Ooohhh – let's go get a drink!" I squealed as I took Bazil's hand and led him to the bar...

"What can I get you?" the bartender asked...

"I'll have a Hurricane!" I squealed...

"And for you sir?"

"I'll have a Nassau Royale..." Bazil answered. We got our drinks and sat at the bar for a while, listening to the music and watching everyone enjoy themselves, and then we got up and started dancing with everyone. As soon as we sat back down, I noticed her coming towards me...

Chapter 17

I started feeling uneasy as soon as she walked towards me... "Hello..." she said, smiling...

"Hello..." I said as I reached for my drink...

"Wait..." she said as she reached for my hand... "Bartender – put this on my tab..."

"Thank you – I appreciate it – but..."

"You're not interested... I understand... is that your husband over there?" she asked as she nodded towards Bazil. I looked over at Bazil and I saw him smiling mischievously at the both of us...

"Yes he is – c'mon – I'll introduce you..." I said as I grabbed her hand and pulled her towards Bazil...

"Hey..." Bazil said when he saw us...

"Hi my Thirst Quencher – this is... what is your name?"

"My name is Dontress..."

"Nice to meet you Dontress..." Bazil said as he took her hand, kissed it, and looked at me mischievously...

"Dontress bought me another drink... tee hee hee..." I giggled...

"Thank you Dontress..." Bazil said as he pulled me close to him...

"You're welcome — would you like a drink as well?"

"No thank you," Bazil answered...

"I saw you both dancing earlier... May I dance with you?"

"That's up to my wife..."

"Would you like to dance with her... my Thirst Quencher?"

"Only if you join us..." Bazil breathed...

"Okay..." I breathed as Bazil took us both onto the dance floor. We were all dancing to the beat of something besides the music and we were both holding onto Bazil. Bazil leaned towards me and kissed me fully and, to our surprise, Dontress pulled Bazil's face to her, and kissed him. Before I could react, Bazil turned to me and kissed me again, pulling me closer this time, kissing me longer... and, just like before, Dontress pulled Bazil's face to her and kissed him again. I could tell Bazil was hesitating and wasn't sure if I was comfortable with what was happening so I pulled Dontress closer and kissed her while we both held on to Bazil...

"Mmmmmm... this is nice..." Bazil breathed...

"It certainly is..." Dontress breathed..."

"Let's continue this in private..." Bazil breathed...

"Okay..." Dontress breathed... "Shall we go to your room?"

"Let's go to your room..." I said...

"My room it is... come with me..." Dontress said as she took me by the hand, I took Bazil by the waist, and we followed her off the dance floor, down the staircase, through the casino, down the corridor, and to her room. When we got inside the room was lovely. There was plush blue carpeting, candles, and chandelier that was dimed, and a bar. "Care to join me?" Dontress asked after she plopped herself down on her bed and patted the spot where she wanted someone – I wasn't sure who she wanted yet. Bazil took his time, surveying the room, walking around, and opening the closet doors, checking each one to make sure the only thing hanging in them was clothes and robes. "Looking for something in particular?" Dontress asked...

"Nothing in particular..." Bazil answered...

"Have you changed your mind?" She asked as she sat up on the bed...

"That's up to my wife..." Bazil answered...

"Have you changed your mind?" she asked, looking at me...

"No..." I breathed. Bazil looked at me and smiled. "Bazil?"

"Yes... Beautiee..."

"Could you get a bottle of amaretto from the bar... and bring it to us?" I asked as I went towards the bed and climbed onto it...

"Yes Beautiee..." Bazil breathed as he went to the bar, found the bottle of amaretto, and brought it to the bed...

"Take off your clothes..." I commanded. Bazil smiled, put the bottle of amaretto down, and took off his clothes...

"I have condoms in the drawer..." Dontress said. Bazil picked up the bottle of amaretto, walked over to the night stand, opened the drawer, grabbed a handful of condoms, and climbed into bed with us...

"Let's get you outta these clothes..." I said as I started to undress Dontress. Bazil opened the bottle of amaretto, took a sip, and watched me undress her. Dontress pulled me into a kiss and then began undressing me. Bazil took another sip of amaretto and continued watching. When Dontress finished undressing me, we were all on our knees. I took the bottle of amaretto, took a sip, and handed it to Dontress. She took a sip and handed it back to Bazil. Bazil took a sip, put the bottle on the nightstand, and pulled us both close to him. We alternated between Bazil kissing me, Bazil kissing her, and then us kissing each other until I pushed Bazil down on the bed... "Lay on your back..." I breathed. Bazil lay on his back, anticipating what was coming next. I picked up the bottle of amaretto, poured some on Bazil's dick and balls, put the bottle down on the night stand, and took his dick in my mouth...

"Beautiee..." he moaned...

"Yes... my Thirst Quencher..." I answered while continuing to suck him slowly and deliberately...

"May I?" Dontress asked as she put her mouth towards Bazil's balls...

"Please do..." Bazil moaned as she began sucking the amaretto off his balls while I continued sucking his dick. I stopped sucking his dick, picked up the bottle of amaretto, poured some more amaretto on his dick, and guided Dontress' mouth to it...

"Shhiiitttt....." Bazil moaned as Dontress took his dick in her mouth. I lay down beside Bazil and began kissing him. Bazil took my face and kissed me hard as Dontress continued to please him with her mouth and her tongue. I got up and straddled Bazil, easing myself onto his dick slowly...

"Oh Bazil!" I cried as he grabbed my hips and started fucking me...

"Yes... Beautiee..." Bazil moaned as he held on to my hips and thrust himself in further. Dontress straddled Bazil's face, facing me as Bazil began eating her pussy while holding onto my hips, fucking me. I grabbed Dontress's face, pulled her into a kiss, and we all moaned simultaneously as we each enjoyed orgasmic pleasure...

"Mmmmmph! Mmmmmph! Mmmmmph! Mmmmmph!"

"Hmmph! Hmmph Hmmph! Hmmph!"

"MmmmMmmm!   Mmmmmm!
MmmmMmmm! MmmmMmmm!"   I   knew
Dontress was coming because she kissed me
harder while Bazil was fucking me harder...

"Baaazzziiill!" I screamed as I threw my
head back...

"Mmmmmph! Mmmmmph! Mmmmmph!
Mmmmmph!"

"Hmmph! Hmmph Hmmph! Hmmph!"
Bazil slowed down, but he didn't stop. Dontress
and I held each other and continued kissing as
our orgasms subsided. Dontress climbed off of
Bazil's face and lay down on the bed beside Bazil.
I got up off of Bazil, opened a condom, put it on
him, and pulled him up off the bed into a kiss...

"Beautiee..." Bazil breathed as we kissed...

"Yes... my Thirst Quencher..."

"May I?"

"Yes... you may..." I breathed.   Bazil
watched as I straddled Dontress, put my pussy in
her face, lay down on top of her, and bury my face
between her legs.   Dontress and I started
moaning simultaneously from the pleasure we
were giving each other as Bazil moved up on the
bed on his knees, dropped down on his legs, lifted
Dontress up by her ass, eased himself inside her,
and began fucking her...

"Oh yes... that's it... fuck me..." she
stopped to moan before she went back to licking
and slurping on my pussy. Bazil pulled out of
Dontress, pulled off the condom, guided my

mouth to his dick, and moaned as I took it in my mouth...

"Beautiee... yes... suck it..." I started playing with Dontress's pussy so she wouldn't feel left out and I started moaning on Bazil's dick as she continued licking and slurping hungrily...

"MmmmMmmm... MmmmMmmm..... MmmmMmmm..... MmmmMmmm....." Dontress's pussy was sopping wet and when I started licking and sucking on her clit, she moaned in my pussy as I moaned on hers...

"MmmmMmmm... MmmmMmmm..... MmmmMmmm..... MmmmMmmm....." Bazil put another condom on, moved my hair to the side, slid back inside her, and started fucking her again... "Don't stop! Fuck me! Just like that!" she moaned and then she went back to licking and slurping. I pulled her clit in my mouth and sucked it hard as Bazil started fucking her harder... "Yessss! Fuck me!" she moaned. She grabbed my ass and went back to licking and slurping feverishly and I returned the favor, moaning into her pussy as we both came simultaneously...

"MmmmMmmm... MmmmMmmm..... MmmmMmmm..... MmmmMmmm....."

"MmmmMmmm... MmmmMmmm..... MmmmMmmm..... MmmmMmmm....." Dontress pulled Bazil in deeper and he grabbed my head as he moaned...

"Beautiee... I'm cumming! Oh Shit... Fuck! Ugghh! Ugghh! Ugghh! Ugghh!" Dontress and I continued licking and slurping on each other softly as Bazil slowed down but didn't stop right away. Bazil stopped, pulled out, took off the condom, and lay down next to Dontress. I got up off Dontress and lay down next to Bazil.

"Thanks... I needed that..." she breathed...

"You're welcome..." Bazil said before he kissed her, and then kissed me. We continued taking turns kissing Bazil while he was laying on his back until Dontress spoke...

"I really enjoyed this..."

"So did I..." Bazil said as he kissed her again and then kissed me...

"I'd like to see you both again..." she breathed before kissing Bazil again...

"That's up to my wife..." Bazil breathed before pulling me into a kiss...

"It's time for us to go..." I said before I got up. Bazil looked at Dontress, looked at me, and then got up off the bed...

"Did I say something to upset you?" Dontress asked as she got up off the bed...

"Not at all" I answered as I started getting dressed...

"Can I see you again?" Dontress asked as Bazil got dressed...

"Maybe..." I lied before I kissed her...

"Good night Dontress... thank you for a lovely evening..." Bazil said and then he kissed her gently. Bazil took my hand, walked me toward the door, opened it, and we walked out the room down the corridor, through the casino, and up the staircase towards the music. Once we got in the room we spent the rest of the night whining and dry fucking to whatever was playing into the wee hours of the morning.

Oprah

"Welcome to Oprah!" Oprah shouted as the audience cheered. Oprah waited for everyone to settle down and then she sat down... "Thank you for joining us. Today, we're joined by very special guests – guests that don't really need an introduction because you all know them – but before I bring them out – I want to ask you to listen without judging – I know that's hard – it's also the main reason my guests have refused interviews – but I got 'em – so let's bring them out – Bazil & Beautiee Osgood!" she yelled as the producer brought us out on stage and the audience began to clap and whistle. Bazil and I sat down beside each other and held hands and immediately all you heard was...

"Aww..." from the audience, which brought a smile to us as well as Oprah...

"Thank you for joining us..." Oprah said as the audience began to settle down...

"Thank you for having us..." I said as Bazil took my hand and kissed it...

"Okay – before we begin – I know you've turned down other interviews – so I have to ask – why me?"

"We discussed it... and... to be honest... we believe you'll treat us with dignity and respect..." I answered...

"Oh wow – thank you!" Oprah beamed... "Now... having said that... I have to warn you... some of these questions are going to be very personal – are you okay with that?"

"I have no idea..." I laughed nervously...

"I'm right here Beautiee..." Bazil said as he pulled my chair closer to his and put his arm around me...

"Aww..." the audience said...

"I love it!" Oprah said... but I have to warn you Mr. Osgood..."

"I know..."

"I honestly don't know where to begin..."

"I started Osgood Publishing when I was 20 years old. At that time, I had five books published. I applied for business capital and used that capital to purchase the location in Milford, Connecticut. I was the only employee in that building at the time – but I didn't worry about how I was going to make enough money to cover the overhead – I did what I do – I wrote more books – sometimes I had nothing left after the bills were covered – but I never let that discourage me – I thanked God I had fans that supported me – and then something happened..."

"Go on... please..." Oprah said as she leaned forward and looked at Bazil intensely along with the audience...

"I was in the office and my phone rang. I answered it and the caller identified himself as Samuel Logan..." Bazil and I could see Sam beaming in the audience and we both smiled...

"Is Sam here?"

"Yes – I'm here..." Sam answered as he stood up and everyone clapped...

"Thank you Sam – go ahead Mr. Osgood – continue – we wanna know what happened next – right?" she asked as she turned to the audience...

"Yeaaaa!" they all answered...

"Sam asked me if I was hiring..." Bazil answered...

"And were you hiring?" Oprah asked...

"No..."

"Oh wow..." Oprah said as the audience gasped...

"But I asked him to come in for an interview..."

"Wait a minute – you weren't hiring – and you asked him to come in for an interview?"

"Yes..."

"Okay – we need to hear this – go ahead..."

"Once Sam got there, he saw I was the only employee in the building and I thought he was going to leave – but instead – he sat down, he showed me his resume, and he told me if I have him a chance he'd help me grow my company – so I hired him as my Vice President & CEO..."

"Okay – wait a minute – you just said you barely had any money after you paid your bills –

and you gave him the job as Vice President & CEO?"

"Yes..."

"Wow – I'm impressed..." Oprah said as the audience applauded...

"So was I..."

"Okay – you were impressed – you gave him the job – what happened after that?"

"Sam hit the ground running – he hired his wife as his Personal Assistant – and he hired his mother-in-law as our Chief Financial Officer..."

"Okay – wait – what?"

"Yes he did!" Joselyn said as she jumped up...

"Ummm – who are you?" Oprah asked...

"I'm Joselyn – Sam's wife!" she beamed...

"Aww..." the audience said...

"Pleased to meet you Joselyn – is your mother here?"

"Yes – I'm here!" Sheila said as she stood up...

"Okay – that's it – I need you up on stage – we need some more chairs!" Oprah said as the producer brought out more chairs, Sam, Joselyn, and Sheila came up on stage, and the audience cheered...

"Thank you so much for joining us – I can't wait to delve into this – I don't know where to start..."

"Well – I had to prove myself to Mr. Osgood – especially because I told him I could do it..." Sam said...

"How did you feel when you walked into that location – and saw that Mr. Osgood was the only employee?"

"When I walked in and saw that – I got excited..."

"Excited?"

"Most people start a business – they start out small and get bigger locations as they grow – Mr. Osgood started with what he knew he'd have in the future..."

"Thank you Sam..." Bazil said...

"Oh no – thank you..." Sam said... "So – I called my wife after I got the job – I told her all about it – and she asked me what my salary was..." he laughed along with the audience..."

"I told him he was crazy!" Joselyn laughed...

"I would've said the same thing!" Oprah said as the audience laughed... "So what made you go with your husband to a company that – basically – had no money?"

"I believe in my husband – I trust him – and he hasn't let me down yet..." Joselyn said as she leaned over to kiss him...

"Aww..." the audience said...

"Oh my God – that's beautiful..." Oprah said as she got a tissue and dabbed her eyes...

"I still had to prove myself – especially 'cause I brought my wife and my mother-in-law in..."

"How did you now you could do it?"

"I worked in the financial district for years – my wife and her mother also worked there – when they down-sized, they didn't take us with them – so we prayed about it – and every time we prayed, all I said was – Lord, you know I need a job... Amen..."

"Aww..." the audience said...

"I'm... I don't know what to say – you prayed for a job – and you got a job – a job that couldn't pay you – and you were excited to take the job..." Oprah said...

"Actually – what I did was convince Mr. Osgood to hire me..." Sam said...

"Mr. Osgood – what was it that made you hire him – beside his credentials?" Oprah asked...

"When he saw that I was the only employee and he didn't turn around and run... I knew..." Bazil answered...

"I'm in awe..." Oprah said...

"The first thing we did was apply for more capital so we could purchase printing equipment, press machines, etc. – Mr. Osgood was outsourcing these and I showed him how he could do everything in-house – and reduce his expenses..." Sam said...

"I couldn't believe the amount of money I saved..." Bazil said...

"So you started making money right away..." Oprah said...

"Basically..." Bazil answered...

"That's when we hired Joselyn..." Sam said...

"You must have been very happy..." Oprah said as she turned to Joselyn...

"I was, I was..." Joselyn agreed...

"Were you your husband's personal assistant in the financial district?" Oprah asked...

"No – that's where I met him and fell in love with him..." Joselyn answered as Sam pulled her into a kiss...

"Aww..." the audience said...

"How long did it take for him to propose?" Oprah asked...

"He proposed after one week..." Joselyn answered as the audience gasped...

"Oh wow – that's beautiful..." Oprah said... "So – how did that make you feel?" she asked as she turned to Sheila...

"I'm very happy – he's a good man..." Sheila answered...

"Aww... thank you Mom..." Sam said...

"Were you surprised?" Oprah asked...

"I knew they were going to get married before he proposed..."

"Really? How?"

"I believe he fell in love with my daughter the moment he saw her..."

"Aww…" the audience said…

"Is that true Sam?" Oprah asked…

"Yes…" Sam answered as he kissed Joselyn…

"Joselyn – what did you think of Sam when you first saw him?"

"I told my mother I found my husband…" Joselyn answered as she looked at Sam…

"I love you…" Sam said…

"I love you too…"

"And I'd love my grandchild!" Sheila snapped as the audience laughed…

"We're gonna get on that as soon as we leave here…" Sam said…

"You've been saying that for a year now…" Sheila said…

"Practice makes perfect…" Joselyn said as the audience responded…

"Oooohhhh…"

"I love y'all – I'm so glad you're here today – now – Sheila – I have to ask you – did you think your son-in-law was crazy when he wanted to bring you on board at Osgood Publishing?"

"Oh no – they had money to pay me!" she laughed…

"Are you saying you wouldn't've taken the job if they couldn't pay you?"

"I'm not saying that – but I am saying I felt better knowing I'd have a paycheck…" she answered as the audience laughed…

"I hear ya – so - Mr. Osgood – you went to prison for murder – can you tell us – how were you able to keep the company going while you were in prison?" Oprah asked...

"I owe that to Sam..." Bazil answered...

"Sam – how did you feel when Mr. Osgood was arrested?" Oprah asked...

"To be honest – I was afraid..."

"You were afraid you couldn't handle it?"

"I was afraid I'd let him down..."

"You've never let me down Sam..." Bazil said...

"Thank you..." Sam said... "But I also had my wife supporting me and mymother-in-law..."

"This is... wow..." Oprah said...

"Sam came to visit me a couple of times a week..." Bazil said...

"I – you're amazing – do you have any brothers?" Oprah asked as the audience laughed...

"No..." Sam answered...

"Sheila – did you feel any added pressure with Mr. Osgood in prison?"

"Naa – once you've worked for the financial district – you can pretty much handle anything..." she answered...

"I must bring you all back for a second interview – but I must get through this one first – Mrs. Osgood – I know you have your own publishing company – right?"

"Yes I do – Beautiful Publications..."

"Okay – tell us how you got to work with Mr. Osgood – and then tell us how you got to work with Mr. Osgood…" she gushed as the audience responded…

"Oooohhh…" I didn't answer right away – I looked at Bazil and he took my hand and kissed it…

"Sigh… I met Bazil at the Hotel Zero Degrees in Stamford, Connecticut…"

"Did you have a room at the hotel?"

"Yea…"

"Oh – so you were staying at the hotel?" Oprah asked as she tried to get me to engage a bit more…

"I was celebrating…"

"What were you celebrating?"

"I was celebrating… my divorce…" I answered as the audience gasped…

"Your divorce? You were married before?"

"Yes…" I sighed…

"Okay – so you were celebrating your divorce – and Mr. Osgood came into the lobby?" Oprah asked, making another attempt to engage me. I looked at Bazil again as I started crying…

"I'm here…" he whispered as he kissed me…

"Are you okay?" Oprah asked as the audience got quiet…

"I am now…" I answered as Oprah handed me a tissue…

"Oh — so you weren't okay the night you met?"

"No... I was drunk... and I was in a lot of pain..."

"I'm confused — you said you were celebrating your divorce..."

"I was... and then he found me... and... he..." I said as I started crying again... and Bazil held me...

"Oh my God — what happened?" Oprah asked. I could see she was shocked but she was also concerned...

"I was drinking... and he came up behind me... he took the glass from me... and... he... broke it... on my head..." I cried as Bazil held me and started crying too...

"Oh my God — Mrs. Osgood — I'm so sorry..." Joselyn said as she teared up...

"Wait — I can't..." Oprah said...

"He dragged me from the bar... to the elevators... he slapped me... he threw me to the floor... he kicked me... he got down on the floor... he punched me..."

"Stop — I can't — you're in a hotel — cameras all over the place — nobody called the police — nobody tried to help you?" Oprah asked...

"The bartender tried to help me..."

"Thank God..."

"He came from behind the bar... he tried to pull him off me... but Billie laughed and threw him to the floor..."

"Did the police come?"

"I don't know..."

"You don't know? I don't understand..."

"After Billie threw the bartender to the floor Billie ran... the bartender got up and helped me up..."

"He's a hero..." Oprah said as the audience applauded...

"I went back to the bar... I kept drinking... Bazil came in... he saw me... he came over... I woke up in his room... I didn't remember what happened... I asked him if he hurt me..."

"Oh my God – what in the world made you think Mr. Osgood hurt you?"

"I had on a robe – and nothing else – he came over to check my head to see if I needed stitches – and he told me he was sorry..." I answered as the audience gasped..." Oprah fell back in her seat. We all waited until she gathered herself and then she continued...

"I guess you know he didn't hurt you – but..."

"I asked if we made love – he said we didn't..."

"And you believed him?"

"Yes..."

"Audience – do you believe him?"

"Yes..."

"No..."

"Hell no!"

"Okay – by a show of hands – how many believe Mr. Osgood?" Oprah was surprised that the majority of her audience believed Bazil and we both smiled...

"Okay – why do you believe Mr. Osgood?" Oprah asked as the producer ran to the first person that stood up and gave her a microphone...

"Look how he's comforting her – he's crying with her – they're happily married and he still can't bear to see her hurt!" the woman answered...

"What's your name?" the producer asked...

"LaShonda Johnson..."

"Thank you LaShonda..." the producer said...

"Alright – you have a point – but I have to ask – Mr. Osgood – if you didn't make love that night – why was she naked?" Bazil looked at me to get my consent...

"It's okay – go ahead..." I whispered...

"I wanted to make love to her – but she told me she needed to take a shower. I told her I'd join her and she was okay with that but when I undressed her..." he said as he started tearing up... "She was bruised really bad..." Oprah got some more tissues, dabbed her eyes, and Bazil continued... "I undressed her, I led her into the shower, I started washing her hair... and I cut myself..." he said as the audience gasped...

"Wait – you cut yourself? How?"

"She had glass in her hair..." Bazil answered as he teared up and the audience gasped along with Sheila, Sam, and Joselyn...

"I checked her scalp to see if the needed stitches... we finished in the shower... I put the robe on her... we went to bed... and I held her all night..."

"Aww..." the audience said as Sam, Joselyn, Sheila, and Oprah dabbed their eyes with tissues...

"Do you have any brothers?" Oprah asked as the audience laughed...

"No..." Bazil answered...

"I asked Bazil if he hurt me and he told me he could never hurt me because he loved me..." I sighed...

"I love you..." Bazil whispered...

"I love you too..." I whispered...

"Aww..." everyone said...

"So you didn't make love?" Oprah asked...

"We made love..." I gushed as Bazil put his arm around me and pulled me to him...

"Mrs. Osgood – I understand how you felt in that moment – but did you really believe he fell in love with you overnight?"

"He asked me to marry him..." I answered as the audience gasped...

"Wait – what?"

"He asked me to marry him – and I said yes..." I answered as everyone gasped...

"Oh wow – so you knew this man for not even 24 hours – and you said yes – was the ink dry on your divorce papers?" she snapped...

"Not that it's relevant – 'cause it's not – but to answer your question – I divorced Billie and he was served before he was released from prison..." I answered as everyone gasped...

"I'm sorry – that came out wrong..."

"No it didn't – but don't worry about it..." I said...

"How long was he in prison?"

"I'm done talking about him..."

"Okay – let's talk about MaryJane LaRue..." Oprah said, hoping she'd catch me off guard...

"As I mentioned earlier – I have my own publishing company – Beautiful Publications..."

"What kind of books do you publish?"

"Erotic Fiction..."

"Ooohhh..." the audience said...

"The first book in my series, 'How Far Are You Willing To Go? Murder Is Just The Beginning' is free on amazon..." I said as the audience applauded...

"That's nice..." Oprah said...

"I wanted to work with my husband but I wanted to keep my publishing company so I did – Osgood Publishing is the parent company and Beautiful Publications is underneath..." I explained as the audience responded...

"Oooohhh..."

"Okay – so you went to work with your husband – what happened?"

"I was so happy..." I sighed... "When I first got there, my husband introduced me to everyone – but Joselyn took to me right away..." I answered as Joselyn smiled...

"How so?"

"She was happy to meet me – she was really nice to me – she showed me around, took me to the cafeteria, and made us coffee..." I sighed...

"That's nice – that must've made you feel welcomed..."

"Yes it did – until I went to the ladies room...

"What happened in the ladies room?"

"I was going to open the door and go in – but I heard MaryJane LaRue talking to Joselyn..."

"What did she say?"

"She told Joselyn she worked there too long to let a Bitch come take her place – and she was gonna have to check me like she checked his first wife..." I answered as the audience gasped...

"Oh hell no!" Oprah blurted out...

"Sheila was there..." I added...

"Sheila – how did that make you feel?"

"I never liked her..."

"Why not?"

"She walked around like she owned the place – and she passed most of her work to my daughter..."

"Mr. Osgood – was there something going on between you and MaryJane LaRue?"

"Yes..." Bazil answered as the audience gasped...

"Mrs. Osgood – you're back from your honeymoon – you're still in the clouds – you go to work with your husband – you hear her in the bathroom – what did you think?"

"I went to go talk to my husband – and she was in the office trying to suck his dick!" I answered as everyone gasped...

"I did not know that!" Sheila snapped...

"Neither did we!" Joselyn snapped...

"You weren't supposed to..." I said...

"No wonder you threw her out the way you did..." Sheila said...

"Mrs. Osgood – what did you do?"

"I walked into the office – I snatched her by her hair – I dragged her out the office, dragged her down the hallway, and threw her out the fuckin' front door!" I snapped as the audience cheered...

"Mr. Osgood..." Oprah started to say...

"It was over before I got married..." Bazil answered...

"Did she ever come back?"

"I told her if I caught her on the premises or near my husband again I'd kill her..."

"Oh my God – you said you'd kill her?"

"Yes..." I answered as the audience gasped...

"Wow – your first day on the job – I can't imagine..."

"Exactly..."

"Mrs. Osgood – how did you go from your Honeymoon – to Hell?"

"From my Honeymoon – to Hell – I like how you put that..." I laughed. Everyone was quiet... "I wound up in hell by inviting someone over for a threesome that turned into a foursome – that turned into two murders and an attempted murder..." I answered as everyone gasped...

"Wait – let me get this straight – you invited someone over for a threesome – it turned into a foursome – two people were killed – and you attempted to kill someone else?" Oprah asked...

"Not exactly..."

"Can we go to commercial?" Oprah asked...

"Sure..." the producer answered...

"Good – 'cause I gotta pee..." she said as she jumped up out her chair and the audience laughed...

"C'mon y'all – let's go pee!" I said as we all jumped up and followed Oprah off stage to the bathroom...

"The commercials don't last that long – be quick..." Oprah said as we all went into the bathroom...

"They don't have a men's room?" Sam asked...

"Pick a stall, close the door, and go!" Oprah ordered...

"Yes Maam..." Sam laughed as he did as he was told and we also chose a stall, closed the door, and peed. When we were done, we came out the stalls, washed our hands, and followed Oprah back on stage as the director cued us back in...

"Welcome back – before we went to commercial, Mrs. Osgood was telling us how she went from her Honeymoon to Hell – go ahead Mrs. Osgood. I looked at Bazil...

"I'm sorry..." I whispered. Oprah watched as Bazil took my hand and kissed it... "I left my husband for about a week... during that time... I sought comfort in Sonia's arms..." I said as everyone gasped...

"So you left your husband... to go be with a woman?"

"I didn't leave him to go be with a woman... but I ended up there..." I answered as everyone gasped...

"You said you sought comfort – did you have a fight with your husband?"

"Yea..."

"What was the fight about?"

"I thought my husband cheated on me..." I answered as everyone gasped...

"You thought he cheated on you? You didn't know for sure?"

"Not really..."

"What does not really mean?"

"We had a fight over his..." I couldn't finish... I started crying and Bazil was holding me...

"We got into a fight over my best friend..." Bazil said...

"I don't understand..." Oprah said...

"My wife found out that I was sleeping with my best friend..." Bazil sighed. Everyone gasped... and then it got really quiet...

"Mr. Osgood... how could you?"

"I know, I know..." Bazil sighed...

"Was this going on before you got married?"

"Yes..." Bazil sighed...

"Oh my God – I can't..." Oprah said as everyone gasped... "Mrs. Osgood – did you want a divorce?"

"No..."

"I don't understand – you found out your husband was sleeping with his best friend – and you didn't want a divorce? Why the hell would you stay with him after he did that to you?"

"Because I never stopped loving him..." I answered as I looked over at Bazil and we held hands. Everyone was in shock. Some of the audience members were whispering to each other...

"So you didn't want a divorce – but you left him – and sought comfort with a woman?"

"Yea..."

"How'd that happen?"

"I went to the bank to transfer some money, I was crying, she offered to take me to lunch... one thing led to another..."

"Wait a minute – you went to the bank – the teller offered to take you to lunch – you agreed – and that led to sex?"

"While we were at lunch she asked me what happened so I told her – then she shared with me that she'd never been with a man because of how her mother was treated..."

"Oh... I get it..."

"She asked me if I had ever been with a woman – and I hadn't – but I was curious..." I answered as everyone gasped...

"We're you really curious? Or did you go with her to get back at your husband?"

"I've always been curious – but it was mainly about me..."

"So you had a nice week..." Oprah said as the audience laughed...

"Yes... I did..." I answered as the audience erupted...

"Woo hoo!"

"I hear that!"

"You go girl!"

"What made you go back to your husband?"

"I missed him..." I sighed...

"I have to say – I see the two of you – you love each other – you're holding hands – I don't know if I could stay with my husband after that – let alone love him…"

I can't explain it to you… I don't understand it either – but when it comes to my husband… he has my heart…" I sighed as Bazil kissed me…

"Aww…" everyone sighed…

"So you went back home – and everybody lived happily ever after?"

"No…"

"Oh thank God – you had me worried…"

"After I came back we talked, we cried, and I told him I didn't want to lose him…"

"Aww…" everyone said…

"Mr. Osgood – you're a lucky man…"

"I'm a blessed man…"

"Yes you are!" Oprah snapped…

"I broke my wife's heart and she came back to me and told me she didn't want to lose me – so I promised her I'd end it – and I kept that promise…"

"Aww…" everyone said…

"Really? It was that easy?"

"No…"

"What happened?"

"He didn't take it well…"

"I guess not!" Oprah snapped…

"He loved me…"

"Did you love him?"

"Yes…" Bazil answered as everyone gasped…

"Oh wow – so you ended it with him – even though you loved him – and you never saw him again?"

"I didn't see him again... until he tried to kill me..." Bazil answered as everyone gasped. We sat there and waited for Oprah to gather herself...

"I can't..." she said...

"After I went back to my husband and we talked, he asked me if I enjoyed being with a woman and I told him I did – so he suggested I invite her over for a threesome..." I said as the audience erupted...

"Woo hoo!"

"You go girl!"

"You go boy!"

"My man!"

"So you invited her over... and you had sex with her?"

"Yes... and everything was going great until he came out the closet... and... I saw... the gun..." I answered as I started crying and Bazil held me...

"Wait a minute – who was in the closet?"

"His best friend..." I cried as everyone gasped...

"You mean to tell me – they set you up?"

"Yes... and he shot my husband – he pointed the gun at us and I grabbed Sonia and held her down on top of me – but she got hit!" I cried as Bazil held me and Oprah dabbed her eyes... "He dropped the gun... he ran over to us... he grabbed her... he told me she didn't deserve to die... but I deserved to die... so I picked up the gun... and I shot him!" I cried. Everyone was crying at this point, including Oprah...

"I'm so sorry you went through that Mr. Osgood – I'm sorry – you didn't deserve that – thank God you're alive..."

"I thank God every chance I get – I thank him for my life – and I thank him for my wife..."

"How... what..." Oprah tried to ask...

"Our neighbors – Keisha & Troy..." I sniffed...

"Are they in the audience?" Oprah asked...

"We here!" Keisha yelled as she stood up. Oprah motioned for the producer to get two more chairs; he got them, sat them next to Bazil, and then went down in the audience to get them and brought them up on stage as everyone applauded...

"Thank you..." Oprah said as she took Keisha's hand...

"You don't have to thank us – we love them..." Keisha said...

"Aww..." the audience said...

"What happened?"

"I heard Beautiee screamin' – I made my husband kick the door in – we ran upstairs... there was blood everywhere – we thought Bazil was dead..." Keisha answered as everyone gasped...

"The ambulance came – the police came – the detective tried to hold me up in the room!" Troy added...

'So Bazil wasn't dead – oh thank God!" Oprah said...

"I died in the hospital..." Bazil said as the audience gasped...

"You died in the hospital?"

"When I got in the hospital they took my husband in for surgery – they took pictures of me – they swabbed me – and got mad because I refused to do a rape kit..."

"Wait a minute – nobody said anything about rape – why'd they want to do a rape kit?"

"Exactly..." I sighed...

"I came out of surgery... I was in a medically-induced coma for three months..." Bazil said...

"What a minute – I thought you died?" Oprah asked...

"I came out of the coma... I made love to my wife... and then... I died..." Bazil answered as everyone gasped and Oprah cried...

"Oh my God – you were in a coma – you came out the coma – you made love to your wife – then you died?"

"Yes... and my wife died right after I did..." Bazil said as everyone gasped...

"Your husband died – then you died?"

"As soon as the doctor pronounced him dead I dropped dead right there..." I answered...

"In the hospital?"

"In the hospital..."

"Oh my God – it's a miracle..."

"I followed the light – I called out to my husband – he answered me – I caught up to him – he told me to go back but I refused..." I said as everyone gasped...

"Wait – you followed your husband – into the light?"

"Yes – I told him I made him a promise – I promised to love him forever..." I said as everyone started crying...

"Oh my God – I love y'all..." Oprah said as she grabbed some tissues...

"We saw God..." Bazil added...

"You saw God?"

"Yes..."

"What was that like?"

"It was a very bright light – brighter than being in the clouds – we saw God's eyes – they were blue like the sky... and they were beautiful..." Bazil sighed...

"Mr. Osgood – I want to believe you – but – how do you know it was God?"

"Because he spoke to us..." I answered as everyone gasped...

"God spoke to you?"

"He spoke to me... and he touched me... I answered as everyone gasped...

"Oh my God – what'd he say?"

"God wanted me to go back but I didn't want to leave my Bazil so God picked up my head by my chin and asked me where my faith and trust was..." I answered as everyone gasped...

"Oh my God – he spoke to you – he touched you – that's beautiful..." Oprah cried...

"He asked me to show him my faith and trust – so I let go of my husband and came back..." I said as I started crying along with everyone else...

"I dropped to my knees and begged God please don't make Beautiee live without me... and God gave me another chance..." Bazil added as we held each other and cried. Everyone was crying. Oprah got up out her chair and hugged us followed by Keisha, Troy, Sam, Joselyn, and Sheila as the audience applauded. After we all got our composure, Oprah sat back down along with Keisha, Troy, Sam, Joselyn, and Sheila and then she continued...

"In all my years of doing this show..." she said as she dabbed her eyes... "I've never met anybody like you two..."

"It doesn't end there..." Bazil said...

"What else?" Oprah asked as she threw up her hands...

"We went back to work... and I was arrested for a double homicide and the attempted murder of my husband..." I sighed... as everyone gasped...

"I won't forget that day..." Joselyn added...

"What happened?" Oprah asked...

They called the office to ask if Mrs. Osgood was at work – I said yes – they said they were on their way – I ran to find her – she told me to call her attorney – they came and arrested her..."

"Unbelievable! Anybody with half a brain can see you didn't try and kill your husband!" Oprah snapped...

"Thank you!" Troy agreed...

"At first they gave me bail... but then the district attorney convinced the court I might run and my bail should be revoked due to the nature of the crimes..." I said as I started crying again...

"They denied my application for visitation..." Bazil added...

"Why?" Oprah asked...

"They claimed it was a conflict because I served time at the same facility..."

"Bullshit – what the hell were you going do – break her out – on camera?" Oprah snapped...

"They thought I was going to put pressure on them to give my wife special consideration..." Bazil answered...

"I swear – as much as I love the justice system – I hate it!" Oprah snapped...

"The jury found me guilty..." I sighed as everyone gasped...

"What?! Are you serious?!"

"They found me not guilty of attempting to kill my husband – not guilty of trying to kill my

girlfriend – but guilty of killing his best friend…"
I answered as everyone gasped…

"What the hell is wrong with them? What were you supposed to do – sit there and let him try again – and succeed?" What happened – you're both sitting here…"

"The judge excused the jury, thanked them for their service, and then he said it was the opinion of the court that the prosecution failed to prove that I intended to kill him with malice or contempt and that it was also the opinion of the court that there was no way I could be guilty of one murder without being guilty of the other two – so he set the guilty verdict aside, acquitted me, and told me I was free to go!" I yelled as the audience erupted in applause and gave us a standing ovation…

"Now – that makes me happy – that gives me faith in God – and that gives me faith in the justice system!" Oprah yelled as the audience continued to applaud and stand for us…

"Let's talk about your book, In The Arms Of A Gangster…"

"Okay…"

"Is that how you see your husband?"

"Yes – especially when it comes to me…"

"Mr. Osgood – how did you feel when your wife wanted to write her book?"

"I didn't really want her to do it…"

"Really? Why?"

"I thought writing everything she went through would cause her to relive it in her mind and cause her pain, but then I realized she wasn't writing it because she wanted to – she was writing it because she had to..."

"Oh wow! That's great insight..."

"When my wife asked me how I felt about it, I told her I didn't want her to do it and she said she wouldn't if I didn't want her to – and in that moment, I realized it wasn't about me – it was about her..."

"Aww..." the audience said...

"Mrs. Osgood – you went through a lot – did you let your husband read what you were writing?"

"Sometimes I did, sometimes I didn't – but I let him read the book before I published it..."

"When did you start writing the book?"

"I started writing the book when I was in prison..."

"You had the time to do that with everything you were going through?"

"I wrote when everyone else was sleeping..."

"When I read your book, I laughed, I cried, I got angry, I threw the book, I picked up the book – and then I'd go through all that all over again!" she laughed...

"I went through a lot of emotions too – sometimes I'd burst into tears and Bazil would try to get me to stop writing – but I had to get it out…" I said as I started tearing up…

"Beautiee… I'm sorry…" Bazil whispered as tears fell down his cheeks…

"I know Baby… I know…" I said as I wiped his tears and he wiped mine…

"Aww…" the audience said…

"Okay – I need you to stop…" Oprah laughed as she dabbed her eyes with a tissue… "So – now that the book is out – how do you feel?"

"We feel great…" Bazil answered…

"You feel great? I don't understand…"

"Everyone has been so supportive – I'm not saying I don't get my fair share of hate messages – but I get a lot of messages from people we've published routing for us…"

"Aww…" the audience said…

"Mrs. Osgood – has it been that way for you?"

"Well – first of all – thank you all for getting my book on the best seller's list…" I said as he audience applauded, whistled, and cheered…

"How many book have you sold so far?"

"So far, I've sold over 1 million copies…" I answered as the audience applauded, whistled, and cheered again…

"Wow!"

"When I read the reviews and I see how much everyone supports me and encourages me…" I said as I teared up again… "It makes me so happy..." I said as I started crying and Bazil pulled me into a hug...

"You must've inspired a lot of women..."

"Definitely – in fact, we've been receiving submissions on a daily basis from women that want me to tell their story..." I said as the audience applauded, whistled, and cheered again...

"Mr. & Mrs. Osgood – it's been an honor – and it's been my pleasure ‑ you're welcome to come back anytime – and please take me up on that!" Oprah said...

"The door's open..." Bazil said as the audience continued to applaud and stand...

"Before they go – does anyone have any questions?" Oprah asked...

"I have a question!" LaShonda yelled out. The producer ran over to her with a microphone and handed it to her... "Did you ever try to have a threesome after everything you went through?" Everyone got quiet and looked over at us along with Oprah...

"Yes..." I answered...

"How'd that work out?"

"It was great..." Bazil answered as the audience erupted...

"Oooohhh...."

"Does anybody else have a question?" Oprah asked...

"Me!" another young lady yelled as the producer ran over to her with a microphone...

"What's your name?" he asked...

"Hi – I'm Rochelle..."

"What's your question Rochelle?"

"My question is for Mr. Osgood – was that the only man you've ever been with?"

"Yes..." Bazil answered...

"Anybody else?"

"Me!" another young lady yelled out as the producer ran over to her with a microphone...

"Hi – my name is Stehapnie – my question is for Mrs. Osgood – would you be interested in having a threesome with me?" she asked as the audience gasped. Everyone got quiet, anxiously awaiting my answer...

"The door's open..." I answered as the audience erupted...

"Woo hoo!"

"Yes Girl!"

"I want to thank my guests – I want to thank my viewers – and I want to thank my studio audience!" Oprah yelled as the producers closed out the show and the cameras went off... "Thank you so much – I meant what I said – you're welcome back anytime – all of you..."

"Thank you..." Bazil said...

"You're welcome – my driver's outside – he'll take you anywhere you want to go..."

"Where we goin'?" Keisha asked...

"Let's go to Mr. Crab..." I said

"In Bridgeport?" Bazil asked...

"Yea..." I sighed...

"Seafood?" Troy asked...

"Yea..." I sighed again...

"Okay! I'm wit' it! Y'all down?"

"I'm down!" Sam said...

"I'm down!" Joselyn beamed...

"I'm down too!" Sheila said as everybody laughed... "What's so funny?" she snapped...

"Nothing Mommy – c'mon y'all..." Joselyn laughed as we all followed Oprah to the exit and got in the car.

Questions

1. Is Beautiee Pregnant?
2. Do they live happily ever after?

Answers

The Drama Continues In
Part II of the 'Twisted Series'
Twisted Starr

Twisted Beautiee Tree

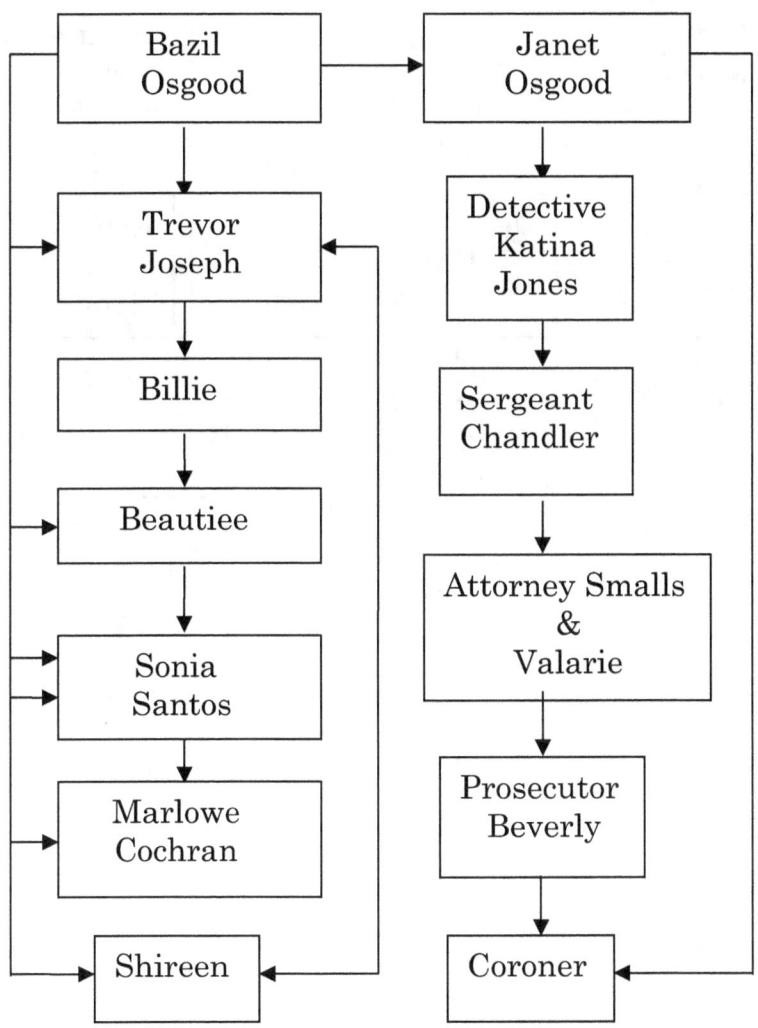

<u>Twisted Beautiee Tree</u>

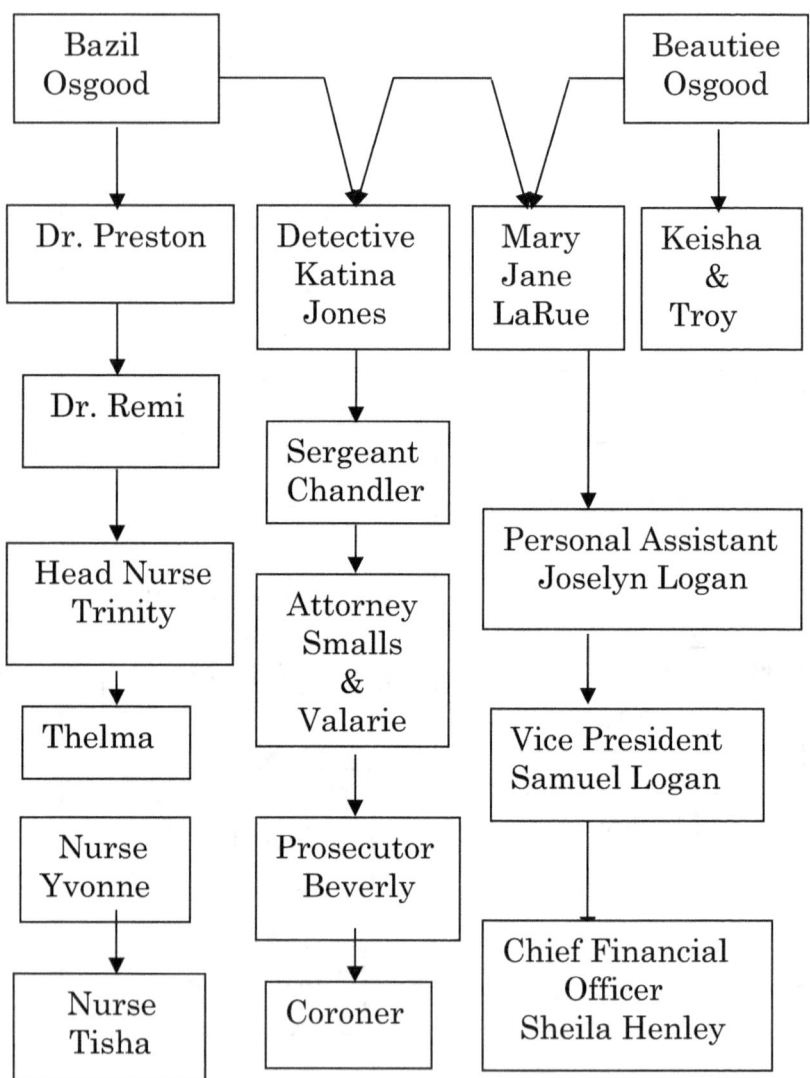

www.ingramcontent.com/pod-product-compliance
Lightning Source LLC
Chambersburg PA
CBHW072103170626
46813CB00004B/1446